Incisions

Barbara Winkes

ISBN: 978-1-0690835-7-9

Cover art © May Dawney Designs

Created with Atticus

For D.

Chapter One

*H*e couldn't believe what happened. This was impossible. He wasn't supposed to work tonight. He couldn't. There was something so much more important he had to do...but his dad said he needed him. Today of all days. He wouldn't ever let his father down again, even if he considered the task mundane and irrelevant, like everything else regarding the business that made up the old man's livelihood.

Dad had been proud once. He was supposed to carry the torch next, but somehow, they both went off the right path.

He cast an anxious glance at the big clock on the wall, the hands of time moving, unstoppable. He couldn't stop disaster from happening either, the plan he'd set in motion already unfolding.

He had imagined the moment a million times, and in his mind, it went something like this: The sound of high heels on the pavement—she always wore them after work. She would be unaware at first, then, maybe instinct would kick in as she realized she wasn't alone on the street, that someone was following her. She'd turn around and try to identify the source of that vague, but bad feeling. She'd doubt herself.

That was the moment when a dark figure would step out of the shadows and grab her. She would fight like she'd been trained to, but her attacker would be stronger, wrestling her to the ground, making her fear for the worst...

1

This was where he came in, the knight in shining armor who had been humiliated, denied the uniform he craved. He would show them. Not only would he rescue the woman, but stop the perpetrator, with his gun if necessary. Of course, the junkie he'd paid a few bucks to scare the woman, didn't know about the gun.

Danny took another look at the clock, starting to sweat when the hand moved to twelve. It was happening right now, only there was no knight coming to the rescue. His chance had come and gone, and he was still sitting over the damn books, trying to make sense of the numbers and the fact that life had denied him another chance.

It wasn't until the next morning that he learned about the policewoman who was in the hospital after having been badly beaten by an unidentified perp.

He was livid. How could anyone confuse "scare her a little" into "badly beaten"? Now he was back to square one. The junkie was long gone, and, with him, the money.

He had to be more careful the next time.

The atmosphere was somber the days after the attack. He even accompanied his father to the hospital once, hoping he could see her, but there were too many cops around. They were watching her like hawks—he couldn't afford to raise anyone's suspicions, not now. He saw them talking in hushed tones, fresh-faced rookies in shiny uniforms. The incident had rattled them, but it also forged an even stronger camaraderie, something he wanted to be part of so badly. They didn't know how lucky they all were.

He was lucky too, considering, because over time, the attack was attributed to a serial killer who for some reason was happy to claim responsibility. The officer returned to her routine, hooking up with a detective, undoubtedly, to further her career. She didn't look scared. If anything, she acted defiant.

He'd been sorry at first, angry with himself and the man who had taken his money and done a lousy job carrying out the plan.

He often saw her, though she never seemed to notice him. With time, his anger changed, and he began to transfer it onto the only person actually in his reach.

The funeral of another young officer shocked the community, and once more, they banded together in grief. He was there, but he could have been invisible just as well, not part of any of it.

He saw her, arms around her friend who had been engaged to the fallen officer.

He knew about this kind of gossip, always picked up on it. Information could be valuable later on. Information would help him do better the next time.

The next time had to be bigger, more impressive, and his timing had to be flawless.

He wouldn't be invisible any longer.

❧

By now, Ellie should have been in a luxury resort hotel room, with Jordan next to her. She wasn't. Jolted awake out of a deep dark sleep, her heart racing, she was brought up short by the cuff around her wrist. Even with her mind still fuzzy—probably not just from sleep, she reasoned— Ellie knew this was wrong. She struggled to put the pieces together in her memory, fragments of images and sensations. The more she did, the more the scenery felt like something out of a nightmare, the kind where a person tried to scream, but no sound would come out until the abrupt awakening...

"Hello? Is there anybody?"

She was already awake, and her voice worked fine. Ellie used her free hand to explore her surroundings carefully. As her eyes adjusted to the relative darkness, she could make out the edge of the cot, the wall to her left, a small window high above behind her.

Not a chance.

She went back to examining the cuff around her wrist which seemed to be standard, the other end fastened to the cot. Not much she could do without the key other than trying to take apart the frame, and with what?

Whoever had taken her here might come back first and put a dent to that plan.

Maybe they were already here.

Maybe they had left her here to die.

No.

She had to focus, palm trees, luxury resort—Jordan. Jordan would come looking for her, as would all her colleagues. Ellie had once talked down an armed man who had kidnapped his own children—she could do it again. Not every person who committed a crime was a creepy serial killer torturing women in his basement...That wasn't helpful, Ellie realized when her heart rate went into overdrive again, her body's stress reaction to the imagery nearly making her pass out.

She shook her head, to clear her mind of the disastrous ideas, to refuse. Whoever put that roadblock in her path, she wouldn't have it. She was stronger than that.

Jordan had been worried that Jonathan Darby could be behind the mysterious text messages, but they had ruled out the theory early on. This was just another distraction, a predicament she'd get out of soon. Ellie believed this because she knew with certainty that it couldn't be any other way—because they deserved their happy ending, and they would have it.

The warm wetness on her face was the only thing indicating that it might not be that easy after all. Her left hand hurt, Ellie realized all of a sudden, and she flexed her fingers only to become aware that they were slightly sticky.

When and how had she hurt herself, or was the question rather, who had?

"Oh God," she whispered in the darkness as the image came to her in a flash, eyes behind a mask, like that other time. A nightmare? Reality? Ellie wasn't much of a believer. She had to rely on herself until help arrived.

⁂

Jordan Carpenter was no stranger to an out-of-body experience. For most people, it was a metaphor when they said they were beside themselves. They had no idea what it really felt like when all you could do was watch yourself, disconnected from your body in a disturbing way.

At twelve years old, she had watched a young girl walk out of a trailer, afraid to look back, afraid of what lay ahead. The voices around her, some angry, some trying to placate, were muted like under water.

A woman, strung up by chains dangling from the ceiling, likely to die if not for any form of intervention. *I deserve to die.* She remembered nearly choking on her words.

This wasn't about her though, it was about Ellie. Ellie was missing.

There was blood on the carpet in the hallway.

"Jordan. I came here as soon as I could. Are you okay?"

The scene was becoming more surreal by the minute, yet she had to jolt herself out of her protective haze. A crime scene unit was looking for clues in Ellie's apartment. Jordan's partner, Derek Henderson, had just arrived. How did he know?

All of a sudden, her stomach lurched as if she was in a falling elevator.

"Why are you here? This is a Missing Persons case. Not Homicide." *Oh God.*

"Officer McCarthy called me," he said. "She thought...never mind. Easy, I don't know any more than you do."

She caught McCarthy's long thoughtful glance and couldn't help wondering what demons she was battling at this moment. Her fiancé, another rookie cop, had been killed during a violent ambush. Ellie was her friend.

"I had somebody call the hospitals," Kate said. "Maybe..."

"No." Jordan shook her head, only now realizing that most of what she'd found wasn't more than a thought, a horrible vision, at this point. "Someone took her. There's blood. Not much, but...what are the odds?"

"We'll see what the CSU guys have to say and look into the cases she worked on. Someone she arrested who might have gotten out."

"Yeah, sure." How could he be so calm when she was about to come out of her skin? Jordan wanted to punch her partner, even though she knew that his calm attitude was mostly for her sake. After what happened to Officer Baker only a few weeks ago, no one wanted to take any chances. Everyone was on edge.

"I'm coming with you. There's nothing we can do here at the moment. Hey," she addressed one of the techs. "The moment you're done with your report, straight to my desk."

The man simply nodded, but Derek's look told her she could have been a tad more polite. Jordan didn't care. There would be enough time for an apology once Ellie was home safe.

"We need to check on Darby—again," she said when they sat in the car. "What if he was playing us all along, working with someone on the outside? Somebody like him?"

"No," was Derek's quick answer. "I'll check with him, no problem, because you are not going anywhere near him again. I mean it, Jordan. The last time it did more harm than good."

It was hard to deny that, so Jordan stayed silent, staring straight ahead into the early morning mist.

"Thank you. Now even if that was true, remember what we learned. The people he associated with were nowhere near as clever as him. He wouldn't do that because he's vain. If they get caught, not his problem. That's how he works, but at this point, we don't even know it's him."

"It's too much of a coincidence. Those stupid texts...We should have never let that go."

"We didn't. We had a couple of more urgent cases on our plate," Derek reminded her.

"Well, this is urgent now. We were supposed to be on a plane to Costa Rica." There was the tiniest crack to her voice. If she paid attention, allowed it to widen, Jordan knew she'd be losing it. She couldn't. She had to believe that whoever had taken Ellie from her apartment was not a smart mastermind like Darby who had orchestrated kidnappings and killings in at least two states.

This situation was nothing like the one Jordan had walked into at Darby's house, and damn it, she had to stop thinking about it. Ellie, eager to prove herself to the detectives' squad, had worked on Darby's case. She'd also assisted in the search for Phil Hobbs, a felon whose escape had unleashed a crime spree and for Jordan, family secrets she preferred to pretend didn't exist. Hobbs was back behind bars, and so were all his cohorts. While his former cell mate TJ Pratt, Jordan's biological father, had reason to hate her, he didn't even know about Ellie.

The connection had to be somewhere else.

She took a deep breath. It would be fine. Ellie would be okay, and they'd go on their delayed trip sometime soon.

In their job, they looked out for each other. Sergeant Bristol would put every available cop on the case...but sometimes, that wasn't enough. She turned away, pressing her hand against her mouth, only for a split second, as she remembered Jensen Baker's funeral.

Not again. She would see to that.

Chapter Two

Officer Libby Marshall was at the front desk this morning, her sad sympathetic gaze indicating that she knew. She belonged to the group of friends Ellie liked to hang out with at the *Code 7*. She'd been injured the day Jensen Baker was killed during an ambush on a safe house. Jordan struggled to force those memories out of her mind as she greeted her colleague.

"We'll find her," Libby said. "I hear they already narrowed it down to..."

"Thanks. I'll see you later."

Jordan headed for the elevator, barely waiting for Derek to catch up with her, hitting the button for their floor harder than necessary.

"It won't go faster that way," he muttered.

"Whatever you say."

In the hallway, they ran into Detective Doss who was on her way out. "We found a possible suspect," she said. "Waters will tell you all about it."

"No. Wait. I'm coming with you. You can tell me all about it on the way."

"That's fine with me," Derek said. "I'll let you know if anything else comes up."

"Yeah, you do that."

Jordan noticed that he and Doss barely looked at each other. Either they wanted to pretend that there was nothing going on between them—she knew, but she didn't have an opportunity to talk to Derek yet—or there was trouble brewing. Neither alternative was of any interest to her at this moment. She turned around to follow her out. Doss hadn't said anything to her yet.

"Okay, spill it. What did you find?"

Doss straightened her shoulders. "Tucker Branson, got out of jail four months ago. He's checking in with his parole officer and his mom on a regular basis. He was one of Harding's first arrests."

"What makes you think he's coming for her now?"

"He said some pretty nasty things in court, if not specifically against her. Takes some planning. He has to get a gun, some-place to take her."

Jordan shuddered. If this was plain revenge against a police officer, it was unlikely that there would be a ransom or any contact. They had to be quick.

"What was he in for?"

"Drugs, assault. He got out early because he turned on one of his buddies."

"That's the most recent one who got out?"

"There were a few more in recent months, a woman who served for credit card fraud, moved back with her folks in Virginia after she got out. Not very likely, but there was another one that sounded more interesting—as I said, there's usually some planning involved in kidnapping a person...and I'm sorry."

"No problem." If anything, Jordan was grateful that her colleagues had mostly stopped walking on eggshells around her. Life went on. Bad things happened all the time.

"All right." Doss seemed relieved she didn't want to prolong the subject. "Waters will be checking in with them. Two brothers, often found in bar brawls, once kidnapped the girlfriend of some other guy they had a beef with."

Jordan wanted to ask, and she didn't.

"She was found alive, a little worse for wear, but not harmed. They locked her up but brought her beer and fast food."

On this morning of all days, Jordan couldn't spare a smile to make her feel better. "Anything else? Derek could go—"

"Yeah. I'm sure he could."

"Are you guys okay?" It was none of Jordan's business, but if anything had happened that would make either Doss or Derek focus any less, she needed to know. Ellie deserved all of them at their best, regardless of whatever else was going on.

"Why wouldn't we be?" There was still a slight edge to Doss's tone. "Don't worry about it. If you want my advice though, dating at work is always a bad idea. Now look at me, I can't seem to keep my mouth shut. Let's focus on finding Harding, okay?"

"Yes, of course."

There would be time for everything else later—even chastising her partner.

Tucker Branson opened the door to them, groaning before they even identified themselves. "Yeah, save it, ladies. You're with the police."

"We just have a few questions," Doss said. "Can we come in?"

"You're making me late for work, and I really don't want to be. You know, work, a paycheck, roof over the head? Those are good things."

"I don't doubt that," Jordan agreed. "You've been out for four months, got a job, an apartment and everything. Good for you."

"Well, thanks. You came by to say, 'well done, Tucker?' Nice touch. I really need to go now."

"You remember Officer Harding. Seen her lately?"

Jordan forced herself not to show any reaction, but she couldn't help flinching a bit when Maria Doss showed Ellie's picture to Branson.

"No, should I? Wait, that's the chick who arrested me. Nah. Frankly, I don't want to see her again. Ever."

"Would you mind if we took a look around?"

In answer to Doss's question, he ran straight into her, taking her down as he headed for the stairs. Doss clutched her shoulder, but her expression was more pissed than hurt.

"Go," she shouted. "I'm okay."

So Jordan did.

Branson didn't seem to be thinking clearly. It didn't make sense to go upstairs if he thought he had any chance of getting away. His irrational reaction made her think he had something to hide, related to Ellie's disappearance or not, and she was determined to find out what it was.

His apartment was on the sixth floor, at least five more to the roof. Jordan could hear his frantic footsteps above her, over the blood rushing in her ears. There was nowhere to go for Branson. He had to know that. The only question left was how desperate was he, and did he have access to a weapon?

She finally reached the roof only moments after he had slammed the door shut, catching her breath. The wind was whipping her ponytail in her face.

"Branson, come on, stop this bullshit. Whatever it is, we can talk about it."

There was no answer. He had to be hiding behind one of the chimneys—there was no other possibility. "We know you got your life together, and you're doing pretty well. That's great. Don't be an idiot now." Jordan advanced carefully, hand on her weapon. "Let's talk, okay? It's just you and me."

The blow from behind blindsided her for a moment, but she got to her feet, drawing her gun within seconds. "Stop running, damn it. Stop!" He didn't, once again not taking the most logical escape route back down but climbing onto the ledge instead.

Jordan felt sick. With the strong winds up here, there was a possibility his escape could turn out to be deadly. She holstered her gun again, taking a brief look at the pipe lying on the floor next to her. *Bastard*. She still didn't want him to die.

"Don't do this. I hear your mom's pretty proud of you. Why would you do this to her?"

"You don't understand! They come around all the time, wanting to talk, they say. Next thing you know, they got a job for you, and you can't say no. I didn't want to."

"I understand. I really do. You know how this works, Tucker. You give me names, I can make this go away."

"You're lying!"

"No, I'm not. I'll make sure you'll be okay, if only to avoid the mess that's going to happen if you jump. It'll be my mess, and I don't want that. Why do you think they let you out after only a few years? You're small fish, and believe me, Tucker, that's a good thing right now. We're not interested in busting you. We want the sharks. Do you get me?"

The truth was, she would have said anything to get him back from that ledge, but to her relief, her little speech seemed to make him pause.

"You promise?"

He made a small step forward, then stumbled. Jordan reached out for him, and for a moment suspended in time she thought he might fall, but she managed to tighten her grip around his legs and drag him to her side and safer ground.

Branson made an indulgent sound of protest when Jordan put the cuffs on him, not bothering to be gentle about it.

"Damn it, lady, that hurts!"

"Yeah, people might treat you nicer if you didn't hit them over the head. You could be a little grateful too. Come on, let's go."

He was more docile on their way back down, where they caught up with Doss.

"*Up* the stairs, really?" she scoffed. "You're the heroine in some horror movie, or what?"

Branson didn't answer.

"The thing is your behavior is giving me probable cause to search your apartment too. You better call work and tell them you're not coming today."

His glare vanished quickly. "You promised," he exclaimed.

Jordan shrugged. "Like my colleague here said, we had a few questions. You just gave us a lot more. Why don't we try to answer them downtown?"

"You promised!"

"Yeah, we'll see what we can do for you. Now get him out of here," she said to one of the officers Doss had called for backup.

"Are you okay?"

"Yeah, I'm fine. Anything in the apartment?"

Doss shook her head. "Not so far. I'm sorry."

"That's okay. Let's see what he can tell us."

❦

Waters and Derek were nowhere to be seen when they arrived. Jordan thought about the brothers who had locked up a woman in their shed because of some quarrel with another guy, but had treated her decently, by their standards anyway. Also, they didn't seem to be too smart about it and had been caught within a few hours.

If only it could be this easy.

Branson had been booked and sat in the interrogation room, brooding.

"This is what you call helping me?"

Jordan sat a bottle of water in front of him. She had brought a coffee for herself.

"You're not dead, even though you could have easily tumbled over that ledge. I haven't charged you for assault on a police officer yet, so be damn grateful."

"Yeah, I heard that before."

"I wasn't lying to you. You give us the names of the people who asked you to do jobs, that will help you. I'd like to talk about Officer Harding for a moment."

"I told you I don't know where she is!" He slammed his cuffed hands down on the table.

Jordan picked up her cup, leaned back in her chair and waited.

"Okay," Branson relented. "I don't know what happened to her, and I don't care. Yeah, I was pissed, so what? It's her first week on the job, and she's busting me, gloating to her co-workers about it."

"You called her names in court. The judge nearly threw you out of the courtroom?"

"I was stupid, okay?"

Jordan didn't share her thoughts, that he hadn't acted very smart in the present either. "Why did you run? What kind of job have you been offered?"

He shrugged. "You know, business. Some meth, somebody wanting a gun...They know when you're just out, they can smell it."

"Anybody threatening you because of the deal you made last time?"

"No. They don't know."

"Good. We want to keep it that way. Now, for some names."

"Darius came in a couple of weeks ago, said he could use some men. Since I used to hang out with his cousin, he assumed I'd do him a favor."

Darius was a familiar name, but at this point, it was unlikely that this connection had to do with Ellie's abduction, unless Branson was actually smarter than they thought.

"Keep going," she said, jotting down the names he included in his narrative. This was interesting information for the Narcotics unit, at best.

As for Ellie's whereabouts, they had nothing.

Chapter Three

Ellie guessed that several hours must have passed. She hadn't made any progress in getting out of the cuffs or finding anything nearby that could have helped her. She still couldn't remember how she had gotten from her bed to this place, and she was angry and upset about it in equal measures...This was a disturbing reminder of the night Darby had paid her a visit. Of course, she had never been his real target, but you couldn't trust somebody like him—or the person who had taken her from her apartment.

Her eyes had long adjusted to the darkness. There was nothing much to see, a black square where she assumed the window, covered up with some carton. Along with the cot, a small table sat against the other wall. The room was tiny, claustrophobic, maybe a closet even.

Who had done this?

She pulled at the cuff once more, as if that could have made a difference.

There was a small noise. Ellie sat up straight, staying very still as she identified the sound as a key in a lock, a door opening. Footsteps, someone...whistling?

Maybe she could reason with him. Of course, the setup showed considerable criminal energy, but there had to be a way, any way out of this. She refused to wait around and see what he was planning to do.

There were other sounds now, of drawers and cabinets opening and closing. He was doing something in the kitchen, she realized. Hopefully cooking something, not sharpening the steak knives for other reasons.

Stop it.

She was going to convince him to let her go, and then she was going to sue the jerk for the price of the plane ticket they'd never get back. Ellie listened, tense, until the footsteps neared. She sat up even straighter, back against the wall. That was as far as she could go. From here, she had to see what he'd give her to work with.

The door opened, and she blinked against the daylight coming in from another room. The dark shape in the doorway moved closer silently.

"Who are you? Why am I here?"

There was no answer.

Ellie saw that he was wearing a ski mask, feeling light-headed immediately. It couldn't be. That had been Darby, and he was behind bars.

"Did you send the texts?"

He didn't say anything, obviously not in a hurry to have a conversation. This wasn't good.

He carried a tray with him, the smells of coffee and toast out of place, but her empty stomach took notice. He carefully set it down on the bed next to her but stayed out of her reach as he switched on a lamp on the wall. Ellie cast a quick glance at the plate, toast, eggs, a few slices of tomato.

"That looks good. Thanks."

She thought she'd seen him nod, but with his gear and the light behind him, Ellie couldn't be sure. Was this his game, trying to intimidate her with silence?

The man who attacked her on the street hadn't been silent. He'd snarled at her to stop struggling. Was he worried she'd recognize his voice? The thoughts were tumbling over one another in her head.

If he tried to keep his identity from her, did that mean he wouldn't harm her? Kill her?

"Look." Ellie cleared her throat when the word came out in a too high pitch. She needed to stay calm. "I see you won't talk to me, but you can listen to me, right? That's the least you can do for me. I'm not sure you know, but I'm a police officer. My colleagues are looking for me." She was making a judgment call by telling him that. Ellie hoped that the criminal in front of her was working alone and low-level enough to be intimidated by the information. Everything about her predicament seemed to point to that. If she was wrong, he might kill her right away. "If you let me go, hey, I never saw your face. I can't describe you. You could even drop me off somewhere. I couldn't tell where this place was. You could get away."

The man shrugged and shook his head as if apologizing.

Ellie was not in the mood.

"Damn it, talk to me," she yelled, flinging the tray at him with her free hand. He had tried to sidestep the attack, but a bit of the eggs stuck to his sweater now, the coffee spilling on the floor. He turned around and walked out of the room.

"Hey!"

Damn, what did you have to do that for? Ellie berated herself, starting to shake as she waited for his return, from anger, from fear. What would he do now? Hit her? Something worse?

When he walked back into a room, he was carrying a dustpan, a brush and a roll of paper towels, quietly cleaning up the mess.

"Okay. I'm sorry about that. Can we start over?"

The man coughed as if hiding a laugh. He was making fun of her.

"Not funny. Please, think about what I said. The longer you wait, the more likely that they will find me. You already drugged and abducted me. If you don't do anything for yourself now, you're going to go away for a very long time."

The sad thing was he had reason to mock her. All her threats were utterly empty. She had only one free hand, and as long as he carefully avoided all closer contact, she couldn't even try anything. Ellie knew her situation was precarious. She refused to believe it was hopeless. Things happened for a reason. Jordan had made it out of Darby's basement, and Ellie would be okay, too, if only because they had finally overcome all the obstacles to be together. They were meant to be.

Then again, Kate and Jensen had certainly thought the same.

The man had finished cleaning up, left for a short time and then came back again.

"I'm really sorry," Ellie tried once more. "I could eat. I swear I'm not going to do that again."

He stood for a moment, as if trying to decide whether she could be trusted, then he walked away, locking the door, and plunging her back into darkness.

Danny wasn't at all surprised at her reaction. He had read about the attack in the newspaper, knew that she had fought, at first, anyway. He knew he had to be careful, not get too close, because she would try every trick from the rookie book. She was privy to all the secrets he longed to know.

Sometime soon.

The world, or better, the local police department, wouldn't be able to overlook him once he had carried out his plan. They couldn't ignore him any longer. Absentmindedly, he stared at the remains of what would have been her breakfast. More like a late lunch, but she didn't need to know that. It was better to keep her a little confused as to the timeline. He wondered if he should fix her another plate, but then decided against it. If she was a little hungrier, she'd be less tempted to throw food at him. After all, he'd been brought up not to be wasteful.

He didn't want her to suffer, but a little discomfort couldn't hurt. Opening the fridge, he looked for a bottle of water to realize that he only had a six pack of beer. He'd need to do some grocery shopping before his shift. He couldn't give her a glass of water because she might shatter it and use a shard as a weapon, or to hurt herself.

After some consideration, he extracted one can from the pack. This might help mellow her down a bit. He couldn't drug her again right away. It was too much of a risk, though he might try later, depending on her behavior. Be cool, make sure everything happened according to plan.

He went back into the room he'd hidden her away temporarily, aware of her gaze, angry, worried, mind churning as she tried to come up with something that would convince him to let her go.

He would have liked to talk to her. She might or might not recognize his voice. He couldn't take the risk. Soon enough, Ellie Harding would be extremely grateful to him. He was looking forward to that moment, but he had to be patient, not get ahead of himself. When he set the beer can on the floor, his cell phone rang, making them both jump.

"Hang on a second," he said, then wanted to punch himself.

He couldn't make that mistake again.

Danny closed the door behind him soundly and bellowed into the phone. "Who is this?"

"Hey, man," said the caller. "Not sure I'm going to make it tonight."

Danny wanted to throw something too, like Officer Harding had earlier, but he forced himself to stay calm. "Okay," he said. "Tell me what happened."

"Carpenter. You have a minute?"

"What do you have?"

Jordan could tell from the Narcotics detective's expression that it wasn't good, at least not from where she stood.

"He had some important information for us. We could make a bust as soon as tonight."

"Great. You came here to tell me that?"

"We had to let him go. I'm sorry."

Jordan had feared that would happen, but the futility of it all in finding Ellie still struck her. Time was ticking. No contact from the kidnapper or kidnappers.

Jonathan Darby was still safely locked away and hadn't had any visitors other than his lawyer since his arrest.

"I assume you'll be keeping an eye on him."

He nodded.

"Fine. Keep me in the loop on where he goes and with whom. I'm not entirely sure yet we can rule him out."

When he was gone, Jordan got up to go check on Waters and Derek who had brought in the Sampson brothers earlier, dizzy for a split-second. She gripped the edge of her desk until the moment passed, then jumped when the person in question stood right in front of her.

"Jesus, Henderson, do you have to sneak up on me like that? I was going to find you. How's it going with the Sampson boys?"

"They claim they haven't kidnapped anyone since that last incident," he said dryly.

"How are you doing?"

"I wish I could work on a case, any case, where no one is constantly asking me that. I wish I was sipping cocktails on a beach in Costa Rica. Otherwise, peachy. They're still here?"

"What do *you* think?"

Jordan didn't share her thoughts. He was well aware of her frustration. It had been a dead end anyway—given how that case had panned out, it was unlikely that the brothers would be this stupid again.

"Okay. Narcotics got their hands on Branson, but on the bright side, they'll know if anything happens. We start over. This has got to be related to the text messages."

"That didn't go anywhere, remember?"

"It can't be a coincidence that Darby is taking back his confession in Ellie's case just now."

Derek cast her a dubious look. "No. That is taken care of." He hesitated. "Don't take this the wrong way, but...You're not exactly objective in all of this—and I'm not saying you should go home. It's not what I'm saying," he repeated when she shook her head, annoyed, "...but you should lay low for a bit. As we speak, her photo is going out to the media, on the Internet. Someone's bound to have seen her."

"Everyone is on the case. There's no laying low."

"All right. Are you aware of anyone we could contact, anyone Ellie could have told something to? We know she mostly hangs out with McCarthy and Marshall, they knew about the texts, but Ellie never mentioned being worried or feeling threatened. Is there anything you can think of?"

"Are you humoring me?"

"I'm trying to find out what happened to Harding. That's priority right now, isn't it?"

"Of course it is," she answered curtly.

Her head hurt, to the point it made her vision blur. She didn't have time for this. Jordan felt guilty realizing she didn't know all that much about Ellie's life outside of the police force, outside of the life that included *her*.

No family. There was this one ex, ex-roommate and lover who had convinced her to go blonde—Rhonda. As far as Jordan knew, she had moved out on a whim, didn't seem to be interested in continuing the relationship at all, but looks could be deceiving.

Darby had invaded her thoughts and perception far too much—women were perfectly capable of committing crimes. Maybe the landlord would know how to locate her...or one of Ellie's best friends, Kate McCarthy.

"There's someone I'd like to talk to," she said, picking up the phone. "Hey, Kate, this is Jordan. I wonder if you can tell me what happened to Rhonda?"

"Rhonda?" Kate asked, surprised. "You don't think she had anything to do with...no. She wasn't so great, leaving Ellie hanging with the rent of that place, but I don't think she'd hurt her."

"How long had they been living together?"

"About three years. They moved into the place after we all graduated from the academy."

"Rhonda is a cop?"

"No, she's in retail. The friend of a high school friend. She and Ellie met at a birthday party, and they were both looking for a place in town. Her name is Rhonda Marks. She hung around a bit after Ellie was attacked, but they had already separated by then. I think she's still in town, but like I said..."

"I'd like to talk to her anyway."

"Really?"

"Is there a problem?"

"No, not at all," Kate hurried to say. "See you later."

"I'm not sure where you're going with this," Derek told her after she'd laid out that last bit of information to him. "The girl moved out. She came to the hospital that one time, but that's it. Looks like she moved on."

"Yeah, well, she didn't move all that far away. She works in a boutique five blocks from Ellie's apartment. If anything, she could have sent the messages, watched Ellie—and if that's all she did, maybe she did see our guy."

"It's worth checking out," he agreed. "I need to check on something. You'll come back here after?"

She nodded.

"Have you eaten today?"

There was a good explanation for her headache, and the rumbling stomach.

"I'll grab something on the way. Later."

The rush our traffic almost doubled the length of her drive to about half an hour, and it took her another ten minutes to find parking. Too much caffeine on an empty stomach made her heart beat an uncomfortable rhythm, and with that came once again the memories. Ten minutes in Darby's basement had felt like an eternity, and she'd spent much longer than that.

She had survived.

Whatever was going on here, Ellie would, too.

She tried to ignore the smell of food coming from restaurants getting ready for the evening crowd and stepped into the spacious boutique where Rhonda Marks was still at work.

Jordan recognized her right away from the DMV photo. There were reddish highlights in her long dark hair now, and she wore high heels that put her on eye level with Jordan who shuddered at the thought of a workday in shoes like this.

"Can I help you?" she asked in a sweet, but slightly puzzled tone. Jordan didn't blame her. She certainly wasn't Marks' usual clientele.

"I hope so. I'm Detective Carpenter."

Rhonda's eyes widened at the sight of the badge in front of her, then she laughed nervously.

"Detective? That sounds serious. Am I in trouble?"

"When was the last time you saw Ellie Harding?"

"A while ago. A few months? I went to see her in the hospital after she got beaten up by that creep. Don't tell me something else happened to her. The girl really attracts trouble."

"Why do you say that?"

Rhonda looked alarmed all of a sudden. "Forget I said that. She's a cop, right, around weird people all day. Things are bound to happen."

"Like what?"

Jordan stepped a bit closer into the woman's personal space, trying to tell herself that this had nothing to do with the fact that Rhonda had been Ellie's lover. She had absolutely no talking room when it came to interfering exes. Except Rhonda hadn't interfered in anything—or had she?

"I don't know. She told me some strange stories when we were still living together, nothing too detailed, of course, but...yeah, you don't really know people. Anyway. I need to close here in a bit. What's going on with Ellie?"

"Did you send her any text messages lately?"

"Me? No, why would I? We broke up. I moved out."

"You were seeing someone else?"

"We are closed," Rhonda snapped at the customer peeking inside and turned the sign in the door. "No, I'm not seeing anyone else at the moment. Ellie and I didn't work out, that's all there is to the story. I still don't understand why you're asking me all these questions."

"Ellie was taken from her apartment last night. We're trying to figure out if someone threatened her, and whom she might have told."

Rhonda stared at her, as if in shock, for almost a full minute. Jordan could sympathize—she'd been feeling the same way since she walked into Ellie's apartment earlier today.

"Just to quickly rule this out, where were you last night?"

"Out with friends, I can give you their names. I swear I haven't talked to Ellie since the day at the hospital. She was almost ready to be released, she said she didn't need anything, and I didn't have to come to the house. I think she was still somewhat pissed at me, but...Oh God. Are you sure she was kidnapped? Did they send a ransom?"

Jordan shook her head.

"If you remember anything, maybe from those stories Ellie mentioned, please call me, day or night. Thank you for your time, Ms. Marks."

"No problem. Wow. Poor Ellie. This sucks."

Jordan couldn't agree more. She went back to her car, thinking that Kate was probably right. Whoever had Ellie, it probably wasn't Branson or Marks—and they were safe as long as the police were running around in circles. It wasn't until she pulled onto the department's parking lot that she realized she'd forgotten to buy something to eat.

Chapter Four

S hortly after the phone call, her kidnapper had left the apartment. At first, Ellie was thrilled, because he obviously didn't mean to harm her, at least not immediately. She was even more thrilled because he seemed to have forgotten about the can he'd brought her, and the fact that it came with a pull-tab that had a sharp edge. She wasn't yet sure what she'd be able to do with it, but she liked having it in the first place. As time went by, she was more and more aware of having skipped breakfast.

Having a beer on an empty stomach might not be the greatest idea, but she was so thirsty. She'd take the risk—there was no way that she could relax and become a little blitzed, under the circumstances. Ellie drank slowly after she'd hidden the pull-tab in a corner underneath the sheet, where she could have quick access to it. The beer was cold and not even half bad—around the next mealtime, she'd be more complacent and see if she could convince him to let her out of the cuffs.

Well, in that case, there wouldn't be a next mealtime.

The alcohol calmed her nerves some, despite the fact that she was in a dark room with her hand cuffed to the bed. She would be all right. Her friends would be looking for her. Soon enough, she'd be home with Jordan and...

She needed to go to the bathroom, badly, and the urge was soon intruding on her attempt at distracting herself from the situation. She needed him to come back, make him open those cuffs and...maybe she could get out. Somehow.

~

When Jordan left the station that night, she was disheartened and angry at herself because she couldn't do better, because she hadn't done enough to convince Ellie to stay that night. Rhonda's friends had confirmed her alibi. One of them had stayed over night.

Jordan had five messages, and she didn't care for answering either of them. Jack. Her father had probably heard about Ellie on the news and wanted to check with her. He and Pauline had met Ellie, and instantly liked her. They were probably worried. Jordan couldn't deal with their kindness at the moment.

Kathryn Larson. Behind the wheel once again, Jordan refrained from the impulse to bang her head against it. It seemed like her birthmother had picked up the news as well, but unlike Jack and Pauline, she was mostly looking for something to console herself, and absolution from Jordan.

And, of course, Bethany. Since they were assuming an abduction, she had probably most reason to call, but damn it, if the FBI wanted in, they could send someone other than her.

Before leaving, Jordan had reminded the lab and every one of her colleagues who worked the night to call her right away if there were any new developments. She wasn't sure if going home was a good idea at all, and her doubts magnified the moment she arrived at her house finding Bethany's car in the parking space. She contemplated turning around, but that would be childish. If Bethany could help in any way, Jordan wouldn't take chances. She finally opened the car door, and Bethany emerged from her vehicle as well.

"No sign of her yet?" she asked.

"No." If she wanted to be businesslike, Jordan could go along with that. In fact, this was the only way she could communicate with her ex-girlfriend.

"Okay. Before you say anything, I want you to know I'll help in any way I can. Resources, of course, but if you need a friend, I'll be here for you."

"Thanks. I'm okay. This will be over soon."

"Let's hope so. Nothing from recent releases..."

"What do you think I've been doing all day?"

"Exes?" Bethany asked coolly.

"That too. If you excuse me now, I'm tired."

"I know you still don't trust me, but believe me, I don't want anything to happen to her. I was hoping I could take a look at her apartment."

Jordan still wasn't sure whether Bethany really meant to help or intended to torture her, but it didn't matter. She didn't care for sitting around at home and feeling useless. Besides, there was no doubt Bethany was good at her job. If it turned out that they didn't need her skills, even better.

"Okay. Let's go."

It was beyond odd, being in Ellie's apartment with Bethany, remembering the times Jordan had come sneaking in, trying to get away from a relationship that had been over long ago. She certainly hadn't chosen the mature way out.

"The ex, what was she like? Did Ellie ever mention anything?"

"She made her change her hair color," Jordan responded automatically, then wondered what Bethany would make of that.

"A bit on the controlling side, huh? What was your impression? She calls it quits for no apparent reason but still hangs around?"

"Not everyone skips town when a relationship is over," Jordan said, uncomfortable with the topic. At least Bethany didn't seem to have any ulterior motives, as far as she could tell. That didn't improve their communication by much, but it had to do. "She sells clothes," she continued. "I don't think she has anything to do with this."

"Hm."

"What does that mean?"

Bethany cast a thoughtful glance at the suitcase still standing by the door, the address of their hotel in Costa Rica written on the tag.

"Maybe she's playing you. Ellie would have let her in, even if it was late, right?"

"And then what? Ellie's a police officer. She can take care of herself, unless..."

"She was drugged? That's what a woman would do, right?"

Jordan shook her head. "There was blood on the carpet, near the door."

"We don't know yet it's Ellie's, do we?" Bethany walked towards the window and looked down onto the street. "That could have been from the kidnapper—or completely unrelated."

"You really want the ex to be the bad person, don't you?" Jordan asked dryly.

"Isn't it always that way?" Bethany's lips twitched into a wry smile. "You don't know a whole lot about her. Anyone can order Rohypnol on the Internet these days if they know where to look."

"She left Ellie."

"Maybe that was because Ellie was straying? All right, moving on. You said there was nothing on the arrests."

"For now. I haven't ruled out Branson yet. He threatened her in court. Narcotics are tagging him as we speak."

Bethany made a non-committal sound as she turned and walked into the bedroom. Jordan followed her, face flushing with an emotion she didn't care to decipher at the moment.

"She wanted to go home for a few hours, clean up a bit before we left. I should have convinced her to stay...or go with her, damn it."

"We're talking about someone who knows her routines well. Definitely knew about the trip, maybe even overheard you talking about it, someone who gets to see her everyday. They would have found another way."

Bethany carried on as if she was unaware Jordan was on the verge of breaking down. Of course she knew. Jordan would give her credit for not mentioning it—that was almost a first.

"Come on. You're talking about cops."

"Your point? No, I don't think anyone from this division did it. I've come to know you guys quite well." She put on the pair of gloves she'd brought and opened the wardrobe, examining the contents, then opened a drawer in the nightstand.

"Come on," Jordan protested, "you don't need to do that."

"Do you think anything's missing? If someone intends to keep her for a longer period of time, and they had enough time at the scene, they might have taken some clothes—or underwear, not necessarily for the same reason."

Jordan remembered Darby returning to his dungeon, dangling one of Ellie's panties in front of her, a warning that he could always come back for her. Had he? It was impossible.

"You're working a case," Bethany reminded her matter-of-factly. "You need to think like it. If you can't, you shouldn't be on it."

"All right then. There's a suitcase full of clothes by the door. You don't think they would have taken it?"

"That depends. I don't assume they took her to a beach somewhere?"

Jordan didn't bother with answering the question. "You were in touch with Darby. Do you have any idea whom he could still be in contact with, someone who wanted him to do the killing, or maybe a fanboy of his?"

"No. If Darby was in any way behind it, we'd know by now. He'd be gloating in your face and keep asking you to come back. You've got to let this go. This has nothing to do with you. It's about Ellie."

"I know that! I've been wracking my brain all day, but there's nothing!"

"Yeah. Everybody loves her. Okay, I'm sorry, that was un-called for. I'm sorry."

Jordan answered her apology with a dismissive gesture.

"Forget about it. Thank you for coming."

Bethany touched her arm, letting her hand linger for a moment too long.

"You're welcome. You know I'll always be here for you."

<hr />

He had brought food in a brown paper bag, turning on the small lamp on the table. The chain of her cuffs was too short for her to reach it.

Ellie nearly passed out from the smell, the promise of grease and salt.

"If you throw that in my face too, it's the last thing you get," he warned her. Ellie noticed that unlike earlier, he was trying to alter his voice, obviously realizing that the silent treatment wasn't as easily put to use as he'd thought.

By now, she was nearly hurting. "I promise I won't try anything, but I really need to go to the bathroom. Could you...?"

There wasn't much she could decipher with the mask he was wearing, but she sensed his hesitation.

"Please. I think neither of us cares much for the alternative."

Ellie held her breath until he said, "Okay. Remember, I don't want to hurt you, but I have a gun, and I will use it."

Only if I let you. She waited patiently until he unlocked the cuff from the bed frame, but then he cuffed her wrists in front of her.

"Really?"

"That'll do," he said gruffly. "Come on. I'll show you where it is." Every once in a while, his voice sounded real, and then he remembered and went back to his imitation. Ellie was unsure whether she remembered it, feeling dizzy from hunger and that beer on an empty stomach. After being forced to sit or lie down for almost twenty-four hours, she stumbled after getting up. He reacted quickly and steadied her.

"It's okay. I'm fine."

She wouldn't blindly run and try to get away from him when he was right behind her with a gun, but the short trip would give her a better idea of the apartment's layout and an escape route. Ellie caught a quick glimpse of the front door before he ushered her into a tiny half bath—a toilet and a pedestal sink—and locked the door behind her.

Earlier, she'd felt so triumphant about being able to hide the pull-tab. Ellie hoped he wouldn't look for it.

Physical needs taken care of, she examined the bathroom, trying to find anything better to use for a weapon. Of course, there was nothing. He had taken care of that.

In a fit of frustration, she slammed the cuffs down on the sink, achieving nothing but having the metal bite in her wrists.

"Are you all right in there?"

"Yeah," she answered, staring at her mirror image. He might not have locked the front door. There was a possibility… "You can open the door now."

Ellie took a deep breath, visualizing the way out of the room, a few steps down the hall and out the door. She would have preferred to have the cuff on one wrist only, but this was a chance too good to miss either way. She lifted her bound hands to her chest, and the moment the door was all the way open, she slammed the metal into the man's face. The mask blocked some of the effect, but even so he let out a pained sound, a curse following.

Ellie ran to the door, only to find it locked. She threw all her weight against it, to no avail, yanked at the handle. "Help!"

Her scream was cut off by the wet cloth over her mouth. Ellie flailed, struggling to get free, but it was only a matter of seconds until the sickly-sweet fumes rendered her unconscious.

Josh laughed when he told him on the phone. "Serves you right. I told you she's a feisty one."

"Well, yeah," Danny muttered. "You still didn't need to slam her head against the pavement. Man, that almost ruined everything."

"Right, you did so much better," Josh mocked him. "She broke your nose or what?"

"Of course not." He'd been lucky, in many ways. Still, he resented Josh for messing up things so badly in the first place, so that he had to come up with a plan B.

Danny resented Ellie Harding who turned out to be a lot harder to control than he'd thought. He had imagined that with everything that had shaken this department in the past few months, she'd be a little more...complacent. He'd been watching her for a long time, interacting with her friends, drinking, flirting...She had seemed like the best choice, always polite, always a smile on her face.

"So, when can I come over?" Josh asked. His eagerness worried Danny. He knew that his former and now again accomplice had a bit of his own agenda. Danny didn't like it, but he needed him. Today's incident had made that painfully obvious. It was lucky that he had turned up again the moment Danny had use for him.

"Not before the weekend, I told you. I have to work."

"You sure she's not going to get bored? I could keep her company."

"Not necessary," Danny said quickly. "Didn't you say you had another job? We do it Saturday afternoon as planned."

"Yeah, whatever. You gotta feed her sometime, you realize that?" Josh was clearly amused with the situation. "Man, you suck at kidnappings."

"Well, it's not my first career choice."

Danny reached up to touch his face around the tender area where the metal of the cuffs had hit him. "Saturday, two p.m. I want this done before my shift starts. You can keep your mouth shut, right?"

"Like last time. As long as you bring the money."

"You got it. Bye."

Money had never been the problem, but the mountain of red tape, and all the hoops they made him jump through, with his dreams still out of reach. They had made it so hard for him. If he had to hire a convicted criminal to finally get a few steps closer—then so be it. He'd be listening closely tonight, getting an idea of where the investigation was at this point.

Chapter Five

The visit to Ellie's apartment had made the facts hit home: Almost twenty-four hours, and there was no trace of Ellie. Jordan called Derek, but only got the voicemail, then Detective Maria Doss whom she knew to be on the night shift.

"Everything's quiet here," Doss told her. "Nothing worth-while from the hotline or TV yet. I'm sorry."

This was impossible. Ellie lived a fairly quiet life, not a lot of enemies to make, except when you counted the perps she had put behind bars, or their families. There had to be something in the cases. Jordan picked up the keys and left for the department, changing her mind midway.

There was another place Ellie often went, before and after the attack, and the man in charge might be able to help her.

Carl Roth was behind the counter of his bar *Code 7*, but he called for his son to take over when Jordan asked him for a few minutes of his time.

"I assume this is about the officer who's missing, Harding? I talked to the colleagues in her division already. I never saw her outside the bar though. Hope you find her soon."

"Yeah, me too. Did she ever have trouble with anyone here?"

"You and I know I have a house full of cops on any given night. Don't you think any of you would have noticed someone who doesn't belong, especially if they're starting something with one of yours?"

Jordan had to admit he had a point, though colleagues came here after work for a drink or two. For sure, no one had noticed her and Ellie sneaking into the bathroom that one time. Was there someone so good at blending in, so unnoticeable that he could have followed Ellie from the bar and attacked her? After his plan didn't work out, he bided his time until he tried again?

"Whoever did this had nothing to do with the bar," Roth said. "Hell, I pretty much know everyone who comes here by name. If they aren't cops, they are civilians working for the department, or from offices around here."

"You're probably right. Thanks anyway."

She remembered Roth and his son coming to Jensen Baker's funeral, all of a sudden wondering if the kidnapper had too.

Jordan recalled the sea of mourners who had come to honor the young officer. She had concentrated on Ellie, then had an unpleasant conversation with Bethany. Now she was chiding herself for not paying attention, even though she knew her self-reproach was misplaced. There had been so many people, anyone could have slipped in unnoticed, hiding in plain sight.

"You're welcome. Good luck. This precinct had lots of bad stuff happen lately."

No shit. She almost said it out loud. Jordan cast another look at the crowd before she left for her original destination.

Sergeant Bristol wasn't too happy to see her.

"Detective Carpenter, why aren't you home?"

Jordan had expected questions, and she had her answers ready. "I thought I could look at the files of Harding's arrests once more. It's still our best bet."

"Your colleagues have been over every line of these arrests. What do you expect to find that they couldn't?"

Something. Anything.

"I talked to the ex-girlfriend. That's a dead end, she moved on with her life. Other than that, there's nothing, no reason whatsoever why someone would want to target her. Are you doing enough?"

She could tell from the sergeant's rapidly changing expression, sympathy to irritation, that it wasn't a good idea to ask that question out loud.

"Excuse me, Detective?"

"I didn't mean..."

"I hope you didn't. As you're well aware, this division just lost one of its officers, and we're working hard not to let that happen again. Every cop in the city is on the lookout, and every news station has her picture. You should go home for a few hours."

"I can't." The tortured tone of her voice told him she was chastised enough. Bristol sighed.

"Fine, look over those files again. Let me know if you find anything."

"Of course."

She was already immersed in her reading when her cell phone rang. Irrationally hoping it could be Ellie, Jordan shook her head when she realized it was a text message from Kathryn instead. She hit delete without reading it. Kathryn Larson had waited a long time before she bothered trying to make amends...As far as Jordan was concerned, she could wait a bit longer.

❦

Ellie woke up to a nightmare of nausea and headache. She might have tried to punch the man sitting on the edge of the bed, again, if she wasn't feeling so weak.

"Do you need this?" In the dim light of the lamp on the table, she could see that he was holding up a bucket. Her stomach

41

lurched, but she managed to take a few shallow breaths and not throw up.

She was still hungry.

Carefully, Ellie shook her head. *Bastard*. She didn't say it out loud. She desperately needed to win some ground with him, until the next opportunity.

"Good. I must confess I wasn't looking forward to cleaning up another mess. If you can be quiet for another couple days, this will be over soon. I need you to work with me here so we can..." He broke off his sentence abruptly, making Ellie wonder if he had revealed a bit more than he'd intended to.

"What's going to happen on the weekend? You're going to kill me?"

"Hell, no," he said nervously. "You got this all wrong. You want something to eat now? I'm afraid it's not as good anymore as it would have been fresh, but I can warm everything up for you."

"Okay. I'm sorry about earlier." *Make no mistake, you'll be sorry too.*

"That's okay. I didn't like doing it either. Be back in a minute."

He seemed to have forgotten about trying to alter his voice. She probably had heard that voice before, otherwise, why would he make the attempt in the first place? Ellie couldn't imagine who he could be. She spent most of her time around cops, on and off work.

Somebody at the grocery story, the drug store, who the hell was behind this? What would happen on the weekend?

What if the guy wasn't calling the shots, and Ellie's fate was about to be renegotiated on the weekend? Did he mean to tell her that she would be free, or that whatever happened to her would be out of his hands?

"Can you tell me your name?" she asked when he returned with a plate of food, the contents of the brown bags she'd seen earlier, re-heated. "Since I'm going to be here for a bit longer."

"No. I'm sorry."

"What do you want me to call you?" Ellie bit into a limp fry and winced. Perhaps she should have accepted the food the first time he had offered it to her.

"You don't need to call me anything. Just be patient."

"Well, you're not leaving me much of a choice."

"Coffee?"

"Oh, why not?"

The weekend. In the following period of darkness and solitude, Ellie grew more and more confident that by the end of it, she would be free. There would be another chance to escape, and this time she was going to make it.

Ellie fantasized about a few extra vacation days. Maybe the airline would even reimburse them for special circumstances. She snorted at the thought. Talk about unlikely.

It seemed like a long time. She wanted to shower, be home, sleep in her own bed, sleep with Jordan by her side. Ellie reached underneath the pillow, flinching when her finger touched something sharp. The pull-tab. She had almost forgotten about it. Maybe there was still a chance she'd be able to put it to good use. Too bad it didn't open cuffs. So once again, she couldn't do anything but wait. It was driving her crazy.

The next phone call was a bit more promising: The head of the lab called her to discuss the findings from Ellie's apartment. It turned out that the blood found by the door was hers indeed.

"There's something else I'd like to show you," Anna said. "Could you come down here?"

"I'll be right there."

Jordan was almost at the door when she heard someone call her name.

"Jordan! Wait." Officer McCarthy came hurrying after her. "We got something from the hotline."

"I was on the way to the lab. Walk with me?"

"Sure." Kate hurried to keep up with her. "At a gas station over in Meadows—the woman says she didn't put it together until she saw Ellie's picture on TV. A man mid-thirties in the driver's seat. She says the woman was kinda out of it. She's sure it was Ellie."

"Get her in here ASAP and pull the security footage," Jordan told her. "I'll be back with you in a few minutes."

"All right. See you then."

Jordan watched her retreating back for a few seconds, wondering how Kate managed to stay upright, let alone professional—after all, she'd been working all night as well. Their situation was different though...For McCarthy, the worst possible had already happened, and she was working her way back from there. Jordan had thought she'd hit rock bottom when for a while, the idea of being in closed rooms had brought her close to a panic attack. Darby's actions, she realized weren't the worst that could possibly happen to her. Ellie had risked her life to save Jordan's. If she failed her now, she'd never be able to forgive herself.

Jordan turned briskly and opened the door to the lab where Anna Crawford was waiting for her.

"I don't have long. We got a tip from the hotline."

"That's good because I don't have much. Inside the apartment, nothing out of the ordinary, but I thought you might be interested in this." She held up an evidence bag with a small, heart-shaped golden earring.

"From Ellie's apartment? Why?"

"No. It's from Tucker Branson's. It's been thoroughly cleaned, no traces whatsoever. Officer found it behind a couch cushion."

"Yeah, well, there could have been other women in his apartment."

As much as Jordan liked Branson as a suspect, she didn't see the connection here—and she was certain she'd never seen these earrings on Ellie. She would know...wouldn't she?

"True, but Officer Marshall was here earlier...She swears it belongs to Harding."

"When was that? I told you to call me as soon as you know something!"

"She did. Now let's go see Branson again," Derek said behind her. "Come on. I have it on good authority that he's not at work."

⁂

Tucker Branson didn't object coming to the station for the questions that had newly come up, but he was acting cocky. Jordan worried he had reason. If this was another dead end, where did that leave them? No. He was hiding something.

"Hey, is that even legal? I've been working with you guys best I could. I gave you names. What the hell do you want from me now?"

"I want to know where you got this from?"

Jordan held the bag with the earring so close to his face he flinched.

"It's my girlfriend's," he said.

"Where is that girlfriend? Can we talk to her?"

"I'm afraid not. Bitch broke up with me. I have no idea where she is." He shook his head with an indulgent grin. "Now you want her name, don't you? It's always the same with you, it's never enough."

"The name, yes," Derek confirmed. "An alibi for the night Officer Harding disappeared would be nice, too. Any one will do."

"Well, I didn't have anything to do with that. Man, look at me, how do you think I'd pull this off? Narcotics are breathing down my neck. You guys come by every other day. Where do you think I'd keep her?"

"The alibi," Jordan reminded him.

"Oh, yes, sure. I had some friends over, we were watching TV. You can check that too. I can't believe you're making such a fuss about an earring. I swear to you, I let it go. I haven't wasted one thought about that cop until you showed up asking about her."

"That may be true," Derek said, "but if you know something else, anything, now would be a good time to come clean. Just so we know we can still trust you."

"I don't know anything. Check those names I gave you—all of them."

"We will. Thanks, Tucker."

"Wait..."

"Come on, Detective. We're done here."

"What the hell are you doing?" she asked when they were outside in the hallway. "He has something to hide!"

"He has a point too," Derek said, his calm tone irritating Jordan to no end. "He has been working with the Narcotics detectives. It would be utterly stupid to pull a stunt like this right now."

"This is not a stunt we're talking about. It's a federal crime."

"I'm aware, but you know everyone is on this. I asked Doss to talk to the woman from the gas station. She's with her now."

"What? Why would you do that?"

"I don't know about you, but I'm pretty sure you've been here for most of the night, and so have I. What do you think? We're going to have breakfast."

"No. Derek, no, I can't…"

"Yes, you can. Doss and Waters got it covered. You'll be of no help to Ellie or anyone if you stop taking care of yourself. I know what you're thinking about, and I know you're scared, but this is not the same."

Jordan sat in the passenger seat and fastened her seatbelt, knowing she had lost the argument. He was right, of course. Meanwhile, the clock was creeping closer to the critical forty-eight-hour mark. If the woman remembered the license plate, if the security footage showed Branson…

"How do you know? How can you tell it's not the same, not another sick fuck like Darby who thought it's his time?"

"We're doing everything we can. We will find her."

He parked the car in front of a diner. Jordan followed him inside, wondering if it had been like that when she had been missing, running on hope and lots of empty reassurances. Of course, that time, Bethany had been on the case as well, contributing guilt and excellent resources. Bethany who had offered help.

To her relief, the diner was mostly empty which might not have been a testimony for the quality of the food served here, but at least, the staff was quick and friendly. The comfort of regular meals had made her feel guilty once before. When she first moved in with the Carpenters, she often thought of her birthparents who were most likely passed out in their trailer after another drunken binge mixed with whatever they could buy from their pusher. Once this was all over, she might talk to Pauline and figure out what to do about Kathryn's calls and texts. Probably get a restraining order, she thought grimly.

"I know you're never going to admit it, but I was right," Derek said after the waitress had refilled their cups. "There's only so long you can run on adrenaline."

"Works for a while. So, let's talk about you for a change. Don't tell me you broke up with your girlfriend before you could even introduce her as such. You keep referring to Maria with her last name only...something is up."

"Nothing is up. We're taking a break, that's all, and how do you know anyway?"

"The people you work with are cops too, what do you expect?"

Derek shrugged but was obviously not willing to discuss the subject any further. He was saved by the cell phone ringing, listening to the person on the other end after a quick greeting.

"Thanks, Detective. We're in the area. We'll check it out now. Bye." To Jordan, he said, "We got ID on Ellie on the security camera."

"What about the guy?"

"Doesn't look like it's Branson. He's wearing sunglasses and a cap. They're running the plate."

As far as Jordan was concerned, this was too much of nothing, and all they had was a blurry picture to prove Ellie had still been alive some hours ago.

Chapter Six

L ong after Derek had left and detectives came in for the night shift, Jordan still sat at her desk, staring at the puzzle pieces on the wall. Tucker Branson, everyone's favorite suspect who kept slipping through her fingers. Had she been wrong to focus on him? There was still the earring, Ellie's earring in his apartment. With no DNA, it wasn't likely to hold up in court. They needed more. They needed to find the guy in the car.

A whole lot of nothing.

There were other cases Ellie had worked on, other arrests. They had gone for the most obvious ones, those who had made threats or had kidnapping as part of their criminal repertoire. What about someone who'd been stewing in silence, nurturing their anger? They could stay under the radar, planning for a long time.

There was no reason for anyone wanting to do Ellie harm, outside the job anyway.

Jordan thought back to Rhonda who had broken up the relationship, but stayed in the area, relatively close to where her ex lived. She couldn't put her finger on it, but something about the woman didn't sit well with her.

She finally left the department and drove to Rhonda Marks's new address, one of the newer condo buildings that had popped up in the past few years. The units here were for sale only, making her wonder what kind of income sources Rhonda had besides her job. Unless she was the manager or even the owner, she was unlikely to make the kind of money to afford living here.

Jordan sat in her car for twenty minutes, then forty-five, not sure what she hoped to accomplish here. Rhonda had an alibi, and for all appearances, she had moved on, unless...she hadn't. Jordan quickly hid out of sight when a car arrived and Rhonda emerged, together with a man. He tried to kiss her, but she resisted, pulled back and spoke to him, her posture tense and angry. She took her keys out of her purse and headed for the entrance. He followed her, grabbing her arm, and Jordan decided she'd seen enough.

She left her car, crossing the street in quick strides.

"Hello, Ms. Marks. Is everything okay?"

"None of your business," the man sneered. "Get lost."

"Oh, but you're making it my business." His expression became weary when she identified herself. "You called the cops on me?" he addressed Rhonda. "I should have known. You're a fucking—"

"Shut up!" she yelled at him. "I want nothing to do with you anymore. Don't ever show up here again."

"I wouldn't if anyone paid me," he said and turned to walk away.

Rhonda was rubbing her arm, the skin reddened.

"Are you okay?" Jordan asked.

"Yes, thank you." Rhonda cast a long look after the man, shuddering. "Normally I wouldn't be so happy to see you, but your timing's pretty damn awesome. You have any news on Ellie?"

"No, sorry, I just happened to be in the neighborhood. Who is he? You think he's going to bother you again?"

Rhonda shrugged. "We used to date for a brief time, and he...misunderstood some things. I thought we could be friends again, but apparently that's not working out."

"What's his name?"

"Look, he's not going to come here anymore."

"Humor me, okay?"

Realizing that Jordan wouldn't back down, Rhonda relented. "Raphael. Raphael Deane. Like I told you..."

"Be careful, and if you have doubts, call 911."

She had seen too many of those "misunderstandings" go horribly wrong. Darby had read a lot between the lines that had never been there. They weren't all serial killers, but it didn't harm to be cautious.

"There won't be any trouble," Rhonda said with a sigh. "He's going to sulk even harder now, that's all. No need for you to worry. If you'll excuse me now?"

"Sure. Have a good night."

Jordan returned to the department where she ignored all strange looks from colleagues. No one asked what she was still doing here though. It didn't take her long to confirm that Rhonda Marks had never filed charges against the man she'd seen her with. Was he threatening her now?

More importantly, was he somehow involved in Ellie's disappearance? With the kidnapper's efforts to hide his face from the camera, it was hard to tell if it could be him. There could still be a connection—and there could be a connection to Branson. But if he didn't want to be the one to get his hands dirty, he would need money to hire someone. Jordan doubted that the small jobs he'd been pressured into after his release would be enough. For sure, his legit job wasn't.

Jordan didn't care for the possibility of finding Bethany on her doorstep again, so she took a turn towards Derek's neighborhood. It was late, but not an unusual time for her to come here in the midst of a case. After all, he'd been single most of the time, and Jordan's private situation had been…complicated, most of the time. Over the years, they had become good friends that could show up on each other's doorstep late at night. There was nothing complicated about tonight—she was out of her mind with worry, and the fear that they were looking in the wrong place.

There was a light on in his apartment, so she parked her car and walked up the steps to the front door. She had to ring twice to get an answer.

Derek opened the door to her wearing a pair of jeans and nothing else, alerting her to the fact that she might not have picked the best time. It didn't matter. She wanted his opinion on Rhonda's ex, and she didn't want to wait until the next day.

"Hey, I'm sorry it's so late," Jordan began, not waiting for an invitation. "I stumbled across something—someone, to be correct—who might be interesting for us. I caught Rhonda Marks in an argument with someone she used to date."

"Jordan."

"I know it's a long shot, but maybe he has something over her, or the other way around. We shouldn't dismiss either of them just yet."

"Okay. Sure. I'll look at it tomorrow."

"No, I don't think we should wait that long. I have—"

"Jordan, what do you want me to do?" he asked, sounding impatient. "It's after midnight. I'm trying to get a few hours of sleep here, and frankly, you should do the same. You look like hell."

"I don't care! Ellie needs us. We can't stop now."

"No one's stopping anything. Every cop in the city is on alert, and we'll go back to work tomorrow. That's how it works, and you know it."

"Is everything okay?"

Jordan spun around at the sound of a soft voice and did a double-take. It took her a few moments to find her speech.

"I don't believe this. Have you lost your mind?"

Her words weren't for the woman wearing Derek's shirt, studying the floor in the awkward silence that ensued, her cheeks flushed.

"I'm sorry. I should go," Kate McCarthy said.

"No, you don't have to," Derek told her. "Jordan was about to leave. Like I said, we'll deal with all of this tomorrow."

Kate went back into the bedroom and returned a few moments later, wearing her own clothes.

"I'll see you at work," she said, avoiding Jordan's gaze, before she left the apartment.

Jordan still couldn't wrap her mind around what she'd seen, and what it meant. No wonder Maria was curt around him these days. She wasn't sure whether she wanted to do the math.

"Don't you have anything to say about this?"

Derek shook his head. "Don't even start. You can imagine, we're both not too proud of this, but it happened. End of story. Frankly, it's none of your business."

"The woman just lost her fiancé! And, in case you haven't noticed, she's Ellie's best friend. I never thought you'd take advantage of a situation like that. That's low, Derek."

"Oh, is it? Worse than cheating on someone who trusts you? In case you must know, this started before we knew about Harding. Sometimes, things happen, and that's all there is to it. You should know about it."

Jordan listened in disbelief. She didn't think she deserved all that judgment, at least not after what she'd seen. Derek had been so angry about Bethany's transgressions in the Darby case, she was stunned he seemed to be taking sides now, and not Jordan's.

"Well, nobody died. I won't deny I screwed up, but this is...You can't do this."

"Excuse me if I won't take any relationship advice from you at the moment. I'm sorry, Jordan. I don't want to talk about this any longer. Go home. We will find Ellie. Soon. This is between me and Kate, and I'd appreciate it if you kept quiet about it."

Realizing that they weren't going to talk anymore about Marks and her suspicious ex, Jordan left, slamming the door for good measure. Usually, they had a great rapport, enjoyed working together. She couldn't understand him. She couldn't understand Kate who had grieved so deeply for her fiancé.

She passed by a fast-food restaurant on her way home, changed her mind and turned. It was the worst possible meal to have late at night, guaranteeing a sleepless night, but she couldn't resist any longer. However, after a few bites of the burger and fries, her appetite stalled and vanished when she wondered how Ellie might feel right this moment. Darby hadn't given much thought to providing food for the women he held in his basement. Water, and drugs. Her fingers gripped the edge of the slightly sticky table. Gross, but better than to lose herself in the memory.

Ellie's situation might not be comfortable, but there was no reason to assume it could be exactly the same.

Then why would Darby change his statement exactly when he did, the moment Ellie started getting those text messages? He had no opportunity to contact anyone, they'd checked that.

Did he have an admirer?

Derek and Kate McCarthy. Did Ellie know? Had she kept her friend's secret? Jordan wasn't particularly curious, and with a little distance, she almost understood his reaction. Jordan didn't have a lot of talking room. She didn't even mean to argue—all she'd wanted was a moment to go over her theory.

Because Ellie could be suffering through the same terror she had.

Maybe she was losing her mind—or maybe she was far from being over her own ordeal. None of the alternatives were particularly uplifting.

Jordan left for home before she'd fall asleep at the wheel and create even more of a mess.

⚬⚬⚬

She managed a few hours of sleep, disturbed by dark and shadowy dreams, before she took a shower and headed back to the station, buying a coffee on the way. After her late-night visit to the fast-food restaurant, she didn't feel hungry.

When Bristol saw her, he called her into his office. Derek was already there, and so was Kate, greeting her with a somber expression. Jordan didn't care when the sergeant told her the good news.

"We found the owner of the car Officer Harding was seen in. It belongs to a Jack Mercer. Problem is that the guy is eighty-four years old and definitely not the one driving. We'll see who had access to his car. The clerk at the gas station doesn't remember the driver, no ID on him yet."

Jordan tried to imagine the scenery, shaking her head. "She doesn't remember why, it was a busy day? In that case, someone else has to have seen him! What about the hotline? Was there anything else?"

"I told Marshall to call right away if there was something noteworthy. So far, nothing."

Strange, it occurred to her that everyone seemed to work around her, working hard to find Ellie, that was a given...It was almost as if everyone wanted to avoid that she'd be first on the scene when that happened.

Hope was brittle—everyone was still shaken from the events that had led to Officer Baker's death, even Kate and Derek, she assumed. Jordan didn't like that they seemed to prepare for the worst-case scenario.

"Okay, Mercer is next, then we head back. I want to take a look at Marks' ex-boyfriend, see if there's something...and I'll check with Narcotics if Branson is really such a good guy, reporting in whenever he was supposed to."

"Jordan, come on," Derek said. "Maybe you were mistaken about the earring, or you weren't, and his ex had one like that. Fact is he didn't have means or opportunity. Hate to say it, but he's right. You need to plan something like that."

"Thanks. I feel so much better now. Darby was a planner, too."

Derek didn't say anything, and for the rest of the drive, there was an uneasy silence between them.

Chapter Seven

T he sound of the key in the lock roused Ellie from a light
sleep, and she cursed herself for being careless. Not that
there was anything she could do until the next time she was out
of those cuffs and hopefully close enough to the door. She was
certain she could outrun him, given the chance.

She heard doors being slammed, then the fridge, she assumed. Oh great, more beer? This time, she wouldn't turn
down any food that was warm, if not necessarily fresh, and she'd
avoid getting drugged again at all costs.

Instead, Ellie heard the TV come on, and a news speaker
relating the Breaking News of the hour. 4:00 p.m.

It felt like a little victory to her, knowing what time it was,
not that she could do a whole lot about it. It was even more
important to stay conscious.

The disembodied voice felt comforting, like a connection to
the outside world. Ellie got even more excited when the local
news station issued a missing persons alert.

"The vehicle possibly used in the abduction..."

"Damn it," she swore. The bastard had changed the channel
to some reality show, laughing obnoxiously loud to something
happening on the screen. Ellie flinched. He was drinking. That
would be all right if she had any chance to steal out of the

door somehow, but bad for her should the alcohol lower any inhibitions he might have.

So far, he'd acted controlled, cleaned up the mess she'd made, drugged her only after she'd punched him in the face. He seemed to be holding a day job, since he was gone hours at a time. Ellie tried to make up a timeline in her mind, but her memory was foggy. Maybe he worked evenings or nights?

She was so lost in thought she didn't hear the door being pushed open.

"Hey, Officer Harding. Not so cocky any longer, are you?"

Within an instant, her heartbeat in her throat, hard and uncomfortable.

Ellie didn't need to take a closer look at the man standing in the doorway, giving her an ugly grin. This voice she did recognize. It wasn't the voice of the man who had brought her food and drugged her in those past hours. This man had come out of nowhere one night when she was walking home from the *Code 7*. He had attacked her, probably meant to abduct her, and when she fought, nearly cracked her skull on the pavement.

"You..."

He wasn't somebody to argue with. She could see the cruelty in his gaze.

"Yeah, me." Beer bottle in hand, he came closer. "You thought I had forgotten about you, didn't you? Well, that almost worked, until a friend of mine was so nice to remind me I was really mad at you."

"Mad at *me*? Why, because I wasn't as easy a target as you imagined? Is that why you nearly killed me the other time?"

There were two of them. She had to be out of her mind with fear for wishing that the other one could come back soon. Either way, she only had herself to count on now.

Ellie shrank back, her hand reaching behind her under the pillow. It wasn't much, but she'd give it a try if she had to.

With the other man, she could try to reason. This changed everything. She gripped the small metal object in a trembling hand, so tightly it bit into her skin.

"I see you lived."

"So it was you all along. You sent me the text messages?"

He shrugged. "As I said. I had a friend who was helpful, but...now he's at work, and we're all alone here. Funny, isn't it?"

"Let me go," Ellie said, wincing as she squeezed the pull-tab, feeling the sharp edge draw blood. "I'll say I never saw your face. You can end this now."

"Hm. Maybe. What if I don't want to?"

She saw the gleam in his eyes and knew exactly what was on his mind. Ellie wasn't to let it happen without a fight or injury to this man who had already caused her so many nightmares. She waited until he was uncomfortably close.

"I have a better idea on how to spend the time."

"Whatever."

This time, everything would be different. She wouldn't be dependent on the kindness of strangers.

The moment Danny opened the door to the apartment, he knew something was wrong, even before he heard the TV blaring some obnoxious reality TV show. Some courtroom stuff, he guessed, people yelling at each other.

Somebody else was yelling.

"I'll kill you, bitch!"

What the hell was Josh doing here? Immediately, Danny's mind was filled with worst-case scenarios. This couldn't be true. If Josh messed with his plans once again, this would be, had to be the end of their dubious partnership. If Harding got hurt, he'd have problems on a much bigger scale.

On the other hand...that would made him the even bigger hero when he saved her. The only player who didn't belong in the picture was Josh. Danny knew he couldn't go into the room now, because she'd realize there were two of them, and that wouldn't help his mission either.

Josh came storming out of the room, clutching his bleeding cheek. He was sporting a cut almost the length of it, ending dangerously close to his eye.

"Bitch nearly poked my eye out," he seethed.

Danny shrugged. "Stop being such a baby. Wash up—we have work to do."

"Don't fucking tell me what to do," Josh shot back at him, pushing him hard.

"Great. If you want out, get out right now, but you'll never see any of the money. Now stop whining!"

Danny put on the ski mask before he stepped into the half dark room with his captive, keeping a cautious distance.

She was sitting up, legs drawn up to her chest, shaking. Danny thought of the can of beer, cursing himself. Think. It might be helpful to set up Josh further as a suspect, if they caught him with this gash on the cheek, but for that plan to work, she needed to believe that there was no second kidnapper.

"Do you want me to say sorry?" she asked sarcastically. "Because I'm not."

Think.

He turned on this heel and went to check on Josh who had slapped a few sheets of toilet paper over the cut. There were no bandages in this place. Danny hadn't expected the situation to turn this violent.

"We can't wait until the weekend," he said. "We have to move up everything—get her into the new place."

"Somebody should teach her a lesson," Josh grumbled. "What do you want her for anyway?"

"None of your business. Come on. We need to talk about this."

꙳

Ellie knew there was only a small window, if at all, and she had to overcome shock and nausea at those past few moments that could have gone either way.

The other man had a knife, one he'd certainly been ready to use before her captor returned. She had managed to injure him with the tab, but that only made him angry, and he had slapped her while clutching his bleeding cheek.

He had dropped the knife though, a pocketknife with all kinds of tools attached. If she reached out and stretched her arm as far as she could, she could touch it with her fingertips.

That wasn't enough. She needed to pick it up, use it to manipulate the lock of the cuff so it would open. All within a small window of time, and in the half dark she'd spent the past two—or three?—days in. Ellie knew that if only she made it out of this apartment, her chances would multiply, but for the moment, she wasn't close enough to that goal.

The muscles in her arm were burning from the stretch, and still the knife seemed out of reach.

Tears blurred her vision, and she blinked them back. She needed that knife. Her fingers only touched a few millimeters of the sheath, not enough to get a real hold on it.

Ellie could still hear the men's voices in the distance.

She yanked hard at the cuff, wincing at the pain, but it brought her a tiny fraction closer to the desired object. Again. And again. Finally, she managed to pick it up and get back into a sitting position, start working on the lock.

Whatever those men were talking about, they would come back at some point, and she needed to be prepared to fight back.

Drugs, alcohol, and irregular availability of food didn't help, but she was motivated. Only a few feet away, on the other side of the front door, freedom awaited her, and then she could put both of them away, finally go on that long-deserved vacation with Jordan...

It was getting harder to keep those tears at bay, because with each passing moment, it became obvious how small her chances really were. Nevertheless, Ellie kept working, and with a small click, the cuff opened.

She rushed to her feet and nearly took a nosedive onto the linoleum floor, steadying herself at the last moment, hoping she hadn't made enough noise to alert the two men.

The bathroom door was closed, but she could hear them arguing, something about a new place, and sticking to the plan. The one who had brought her here had just come home, so there was a chance he hadn't locked up yet. She wished they had left the door ajar so she could have taken a look at them for ID later. Someone had to have rented this apartment, and those men weren't ghosts, someone in the building would recognize them. Staying alive was the most important thing right now.

She got a glimpse into an almost empty kitchen/dining room area, one chair and a table, an empty shelf, and a box. It made her think that this apartment had been rented for one specific purpose only.

Ellie tiptoed past the bathroom door, made it unseen to the front door that wasn't locked.

This moment, the men returned from the bathroom.

Ellie didn't look back. She ran.

Two stories, the third, then she could see the front door of the building. Behind her, she could hear the men still arguing, yelling, but she blocked out those sounds, her attention focused on her goal. The linoleum floor was cool under her bare feet, and the thought sprang to mind that she was still barefoot and in her nightgown. The minute distraction was enough for her to stumble and fall down the last four or five steps, heavy footsteps two landings above her.

Ellie gritted her teeth and clutched the banister, pulling herself up. She yanked the door open and stepped outside, shivering in the cool air. At the end of the block, she could see a small convenience store. They were bound to have a phone in there. She was going to make it. The thought drowned out all pain and discomfort.

Time seemed to slow down in the moments it took her to reach the door, a bell alerting her arrival to the puzzled clerk behind the counter.

"Ma'am? Do you need help?"

At this display of kindness from a complete stranger, Ellie nearly started to cry. She had to keep it together for a bit longer—the danger wasn't past yet.

"I need you to call the police, and I need to..."

The bell sounded again, and Ellie dove behind the counter.

Jack Mercer claimed he hadn't driven his car in almost five years, and he had no idea how it could have possibly been involved in a crime.

He studied the picture from the security camera closely, and long enough for Jordan to tap her foot on the floor. Derek sent her a pointed look, and she stopped, wringing her hands in her lap again.

"Is there anyone else you might have lent it to before, a family member, friends, did someone ask to borrow it?"

Mercer held the picture even closer to his eyes.

"Not that I can think of. I don't recognize this gentleman, but...You must know, my nephew's son, he once got into a bit of trouble. I didn't say anything before, because that was a long time ago, and you gotta give people the benefit of the doubt, right? Second chances and all. Anyway, Michael, he used to hang out with a guy named Tucker who nearly got him sent to prison for a long time. Maybe he knows something. He seems the type to do something like that, or at least gets his hands dirty. I forgot his last name though."

Jordan sat up straighter. "Tucker Branson?"

"I don't know," Mercer said to her frustration. "I only heard about this from my nephew, and I can tell you, he wasn't pleased. Fortunately, Michael was mostly driving them around, so he got off lightly. Did they come back for him? I hope he's not in any trouble now?"

Jordan didn't think she needed to answer that question. How else would the yet unnamed perp have gotten access to the car used in Ellie's abduction?

"We'll check on that. Do you know where we find Michael?"

"Yes, but he won't be home. He works out of town, in construction, and comes back on the weekends. You'll find him under this address Friday night. Oh my."

"Do you know where he works, or whom we could contact for that information?" Derek asked. "It's important that we speak to him and find this woman."

Mercer sighed. "I guess you could ask my nephew. Good Lord, Michael, what did you get yourself into this time? A policewoman?"

Jordan refrained from shaking her head. As if a different profession would have made this mess any better.

At least the pieces were coming together. They would find Ellie, and soon.

The question remained, why had these men conspired to abduct her? All of them were relatively small players, drugs, auto theft, both Branson and Mercer's nephew had claimed to have turned their lives around.

Who was that third man in the equation, and what was his incentive?

Jordan didn't want to think too hard of the possibilities.

They had to bring back Branson and pay Michael Mercer a visit at this job. As long as they were moving forward, there was no time and reason to despair.

Not yet.

When she checked her cell phone, there was another message from Kathryn.

Please, don't ignore me.

Jordan resisted the urge to text back, *Now's not the time. Never is more like it.*

Chapter Eight

From her dubious hiding place behind the counter, Ellie listened. Ward had probably seen her coming in. The story he was trying to sell to the clerk, confirmed her fear.

"Look, I know what you're thinking, but I can assure you, it's not like that. My sister ran away for the second time this week, she's a little..." Ellie could only imagine the wordless gesture. "See what she did to my face? She really needs her meds. If she came here, I need you to understand you can't believe a single word she says."

She shuddered at the sound of an all too familiar voice. She saw the woman cast her a quick uncertain glance and shook her head.

He's lying.

"Anyway, I need to take her with me right now."

"I'm sorry. I didn't see anyone."

"I think we both know that's not true," Ward said.

She reached for something underneath the counter. Ellie hoped she had some sort of security system in here, alerting the police.

"Sir...I didn't see your sister. You might want to ask the police for help."

"Don't give me that bullshit! I saw her go in! Where is she? You tell me right now, bitch!"

Ellie crept closer to the phone, jumping when a gunshot sounded within the confines of the room, something breaking, glass raining from the ceiling...and then another one.

The clerk dropped the shotgun she was holding, shell-shocked.

"Oh my God," she said. "He had a gun trained on me. He was going to kill me...both of us."

"I know. You're going to be okay. I promise." Ellie quickly made sure that the safety was on, then turned to the man lying in a growing pool of blood, the gun only inches from his hand. Her stomach was churning, but she forced herself to check for a pulse, finding none. Then she grabbed the phone on the counter without asking. As she punched in the numbers, she took the first real look at her kidnapper, white, late twenties to early thirties, brown hair, wearing unassuming dark blue and black gear—dead. She forced back the nausea, wondering why this man had chosen not only to attack her on her way home months ago, but came back for her. She kneeled down to check for an ID in the man's pocket, finding a driver's license with the name Josh Ward. That sounded vaguely familiar, but she wasn't sure why.

The ground seemed to give way for a moment when she heard the voice of the 911 dispatch officer.

"This is Officer Ellie Harding," she said. "I need backup, a crime scene unit and...a coroner."

⁓

It was a long drive out to the construction site, but Jordan felt it was worth it. Michael Mercer was quick to realize he had only one more chance to prove himself as the least criminal.

"Tucker came by," he said, "needed a car for something, and I thought my great uncle wouldn't even notice. What was I supposed to do? Tucker said I owed him, and I guess in a way that's true. They all got longer sentences, partly because of me. He was out and had recently changed his job, needed a set of wheels for a friend. That's all I know."

Detective Doss was going to take care of Branson, and she needed to tell her to hold him under any circumstances.

"Tell me about that friend. The one who planned everything with Branson."

"Josh...I have no idea what became of him, and he isn't much of a planner. He used much of the product for himself." Mercer shrugged. "As you probably know, we weren't exactly career criminals. I was stupid enough to think there was some quick money in it. I know better now."

"A last name."

"Josh Ward. Was a rich kid back in the days, family disowned him eventually since he wasn't willing to cut back on the habit. I didn't hear from him, but the last thing I knew he'd do anything for money."

Even kidnap a cop, Jordan thought. Would he come up with the idea all by himself? Why didn't he send a ransom if this was all about money for drugs? How much did Tucker know?

Derek's phone rang, and he excused himself, his expression turning serious. Jordan had a hard time not to interrupt him.

Finally, he nodded to her, said to Mercer, "That will be all for now, thanks, Mr. Mercer. We'll be in touch. Detective? She's okay," he said the moment they were out of earshot. "Ellie managed to get away to a convenience store where Ward threatened the clerk, and she shot him. The clerk did. Ellie's fine. Did you hear what I said?"

Jordan emerged from the fog that seemed to have settled over her, the resulting relief staggering.

"Thank God."

"Yeah. Let's go see her. I believe Branson has many more questions to answer, and this time, he won't get out of it so easily."

Jordan realized she still didn't understand why. Branson, Ward, Mercer, what was the motive? She couldn't help thinking that there was more to the story than they knew at this point, but frankly, for the moment, it didn't matter. Ellie was alive and obviously fairly well.

She'd care about everything else later.

Jordan handed over the car keys without a word when she realized her hands were shaking. She had to keep the worst-case scenarios at bay, but they always played in the back of her mind. People weren't born good persons. Some got lucky.

She wished Derek would drive faster.

"Would you relax? She's okay. Maria says she talked to her."

Jordan had told everyone she was okay, too, in the days after her rescue from a serial killer's basement. That didn't necessarily mean it was true.

❦

She had not expected to find Ellie still at the scene, glaring at the paramedic who asked her to come with him, obviously not for the first time. That could mean many things, but for the moment, Jordan was overwhelmed with relief just to see it was true, she was alive and well from the looks of it.

"Kate? I told you I need some clothes! I can't leave here now. The apartment is somewhere around here, I know it. You have to find the guy."

Find whom? The coroner had left with Ward's body, and Branson was in custody. Michael Mercer had never been involved in the abduction the first place.

"Ellie. It's okay. You're safe now. You should do what the gentleman says."

Ellie looked at her as if Jordan was some sort of apparition, like she couldn't believe her eyes.

"Come. We need to get you checked out." She carefully hugged her. Ellie accepted the gesture, sagging a little in her embrace. "This is not what I expected our vacation to be like," she said, sounding weary.

Jordan had blocked out most of the moments directly after her own rescue, but she remembered the feeling of keeling over any minute, of having to carefully assess if this was reality or a merciful fantasy.

"I know. We'll do it as soon as possible. Let's make sure you're okay first."

Ellie looked down at herself and winced. Her palms and knees were scraped, dried blood on her leg.

"I managed to fall down half a flight of chairs. It's not pretty, but that's about the worst. The apartment where he held me is about a block from here. I came to the store to find a phone."

"Ward is dead, Ellie."

"Yes, I know. Not him, the other guy."

"Tucker Branson? He's in custody as well. Doss is talking to him right now. You don't have to worry about them."

"Branson?" Ellie shook her head. "How's he connected to this? I never saw him. There was someone else, in that apartment, less than an hour ago."

"He got the car for the kidnapper. They guy who gave it to him claims he didn't know anything, and his story adds up. Branson didn't drive though, but I'm sure he knows what that car was for. The one driving it was Ward...so everyone's accounted for."

"No. There was someone else," Ellie insisted.

The timeline didn't add up, but it wouldn't be so surprising if Ellie was a little confused at this point. Jordan had a hard time focusing on anything but the relief and giddiness. Second chances—between the two of them, they had used up a few by now.

"Let's get you cleaned up and bandaged."

"I agree with Detective Carpenter," Sergeant Bristol said behind them. "I admit I'll be happy when you're back at work, but now listen to your colleague. Let them take care of you."

"I'll drop by your apartment on the way and get you some fresh clothes," Jordan offered, kissing her quickly on the cheek. "It won't be long." She accompanied Ellie to the ambulance and promised to join her soon.

Nevertheless, when the ambulance had left, she found Bristol and Doss, asking for an update. She wanted to hear what Ellie's official version of the story was, first, before she started listening and worrying for anything between the lines, anything Ellie might have kept out.

"Clerk says she came running inside, asking for a phone. Ward was after her. When he came inside, he told some story about how he was looking for his sister who ran away and needed her meds. He had a big gash on his cheek, but she thought something was off. When she didn't believe him, he threatened the clerk with a gun, clerk shot him instead. Ellie backs up the story," Detective Doss related. "We found the apartment. I was just about to go over there. Crew's there right now."

"Okay. I'd like to take a look. Can you meet me after?"

"Sure, just give me a call. I'll be at the station, taking the clerk's statement."

Derek walked inside the store, and there was another one of those awkward glances between him and Doss. Jordan briefly wondered if she knew about Kate or simply was suspicious about their break-up, but this was none of her business.

"Did Ellie say anything about what happened?"

"Could have been worse," Doss said. Derek raised an eyebrow at that, but Jordan had read enough in her tone and composure. It was everything she needed to know.

"All right. I'll see you later."

She had to see the place and assure herself it was nothing like Darby's medieval torture chamber, but she needed to be with Ellie more. So when Jordan was quickly packing a few clothes at her apartment, giddy with relief that this wasn't a crime scene any longer, she had no patience for another call from Kathryn.

Answering, she didn't feel like mincing words.

"Whatever it is you want, Kathryn, you're not getting it from me. Let me be very clear, I'm not interested in your side of things. Don't make something special out of the fact that I saved your life. I would have done the same for anyone. It's my job, remember? Stop calling."

"You're not even going to talk to me?" Kathryn asked in disbelief, and Jordan scolded herself for not hanging up right away.

"I am talking to you now, aren't I? I'm sorry it's not what you expected. Maybe if you'd given a damn many years ago...who am I kidding? Look, we found Ellie. I need to bring her some clothes."

"Is she okay?"

"I don't know why that would be of any concern to you, but yes, thank God she is. I don't have time right now."

Jordan disconnected the call, annoyed at herself for feeling slightly guilty. Of course, she knew where that sentiment was coming from. She'd take some time to deal with it someday, or never.

Real family came first. She had to call Jack and Pauline and tell them Ellie was safe.

Ellie understood that most of her friends had been working tirelessly and were probably still busy wrapping up the scene, the shooting in the convenience store, and the apartment she'd fled from—she couldn't help feeling a little lost.

Detective Doss had taken her initial statement at the scene since Ellie had assured her she felt well enough to do it, and she'd probably be back for more details.

Jordan would have questions too, but at the moment, it was just her, alone with her thoughts after she'd been examined, and minor wounds cleaned and bandaged.

She reached up to her hair and cringed. The doctor had recommended an overnight stay to watch any reaction to the drugs she had been given—Ellie knew she wasn't harmed though she could have been, because her kidnapper had a partner who wasn't nearly as mild-mannered as he was. Josh Ward was dead. From what she could tell, they hadn't found the other guy yet, the thought making her uneasy. Just because he hadn't hit her and brought her food, it didn't mean he should go free and possibly take another woman he'd hide in his apartment.

Jordan would be here soon. She could relax for now, the danger averted, from the weird guy who had taken her, and the other one who seemed to be the hired help in crime, the one who had more sinister plans. Ellie shuddered at the memory of his hands on her, remembering with some satisfaction when she'd cut him. The pull-tab had come in handy after all, and it had enabled her to fight him off.

Lucky.

She didn't want to go there, but she knew that her and her co-workers' best chances to find the accomplice depended on her remembering as many details as possible. Somebody needed to pay for screwing up her vacation. Things had to get back to normal.

❧

Jordan wanted to get to the hospital as soon as possible, but she also needed information, details, and every clue they could get as to why Josh Ward had gone after Ellie—and if there was someone else they had to look at.

Branson had gotten the car for Ward. He looked good enough as the other man.

At the apartment, the crew had bagged Ward's computer, and some paperwork stating him as the tenant. They had found a cell phone in a box with clothes, and to no one's surprise, it turned out to be the phone the text messages to Ellie had been sent from. She looked into every room, careful not to disturb the crew's work. In the small kitchen, there was a brown bag from a fast-food restaurant. The place was nearly empty, with only a few boxes and pieces of furniture. It made her wonder if Ward had planned to move in at some point, or if he had rented this unit with the abduction in mind.

The last room was the hardest, the tiny bedroom, not much bigger than a closet, where Ellie had been held. The cuffs weren't there anymore, but in an evidence bag on the way to the station. Even so, she could tell the story in her mind. In a situation like this, your life depended on acting the moment a chance presented itself. A small piece of metal, a detail overlooked on the kidnapper's side had been Ellie's chance.

Thank God.

There were no chains, no torture instruments in this room, yet for a moment, the image of Darby's basement overlaid reality, a swirling vortex drawing her in. Jordan came back to the present moment with a gasp, realizing she was trembling. This wasn't good. She had to be there for Ellie now. In fact, she should be *with* her.

She found Detective Waters talking to one of the techs in the hallway.

"Do you have a minute?"

"Sure," he said, stepping aside. "I'm surprised to see you here."

"Just checking in quickly. Ellie said there were two kidnappers. Any trace of the other one?"

"None whatsoever. We have to wait for DNA, but so far there's nothing suggesting that anyone other than Ward was in this apartment. He might have rented it for this specific purpose. Less than three months ago, that's quite the coincidence."

"Hm. Yes."

"What does that mean? Looks pretty cut and dried to me. His name was on the list after all. Marshall was main on the arrest, but Harding was there that day. He might not have threatened her, but maybe that wasn't his objective after all. Those text messages...more like he was obsessed with her. Branson definitely is dirty, but his crime is that he didn't prevent one when he could. I don't think he was interested in getting any closer to this, and I'm sure he didn't plan it."

"No. I don't think so. If Ellie says there was another man, I believe her. Ward, he couldn't have been the brains behind something like this."

"We'll see," Waters ended the conversation. "I've got to go, and you should be elsewhere as well."

Jordan took the not-so-subtle hint and left.

The last time she'd been to a hospital, bringing clothes to someone, had been after TJ Pratt had held Kathryn hostage in her trailer. Kathryn had somehow mistaken the situation for a chance at a late reunion, imagined that everything was forgiven. Jordan wasn't ready to do that, and she didn't think she'd ever be. She had no idea how to make that clear to her birthmother, but it wasn't the most pressing problem after all.

To her surprise, Ellie was sitting up and scribbling on a notepad when she came in.

"Oh, good you're here," she said. "I asked the nurse to bring me something to write. I told the story to Doss earlier, but I thought it would be better to take notes and make sure I don't forget too much. Any news on the second guy?"

"No, not so far. Waters even doubts there was another one, but..."

"What?" Ellie frowned. "No. They were two, definitely. I'm still trying for figure out who was the creepier one. I heard them talking to each other in the bathroom when I got out, and they came after me. Ward...I recognized his voice."

Jordan sat down beside her on the edge of the bed and embraced her. They'd been wrong all along to believe Darby in the first place. He'd been playing them, even after changing his story.

"Anyway." Ellie pulled back slightly. "The other guy, he was strange. Didn't talk to me at all at first, then he was trying to mask his voice, but every once in a while he slipped. In the end, he completely gave it up. I tried to figure out whether or not I know him. It's been driving me crazy."

"We'll find him," Jordan assured her. "You should rest for a bit."

"I don't know. I've been lying down for the better part of the week, and that wasn't fun. What I really want is to shower and get into fresh clothes, and I told the nurse I wanted to speak to the doctor as well, have him discharge me. You could take me home? I don't really know what I'm doing here. I got hurt worse playing outside as a kid."

"Ellie. You were drugged."

"Yes. That part sucked." For a moment, Ellie's gaze was haunted, but the determination returned. "Nevertheless, it's over. I understand we can't get on the next plane to Costa Rica right away, but let's not exaggerate this. It's over."

"Yes, it is." Jordan was more than willing to leave it at that for the moment. The nightmares would come soon enough.

The doctor was willing to let Ellie go, which came as a surprise. However, Jordan canceled her meeting with Detective Doss to go home with her.

Ellie was silent for most of the drive, but when they were halfway there, she said, "Would you mind if I spent the night at your place? You got me some clothes, and it would be easier for you too. If that's okay with you."

"Of course."

Jordan could imagine why Ellie preferred not to be in her own home. Ward had been in there, and Darby before. Those were hardly memories she'd want to deal with right now.

Ellie breathed a sigh of relief, leaning back in her seat.

"All right," she said, managing a smile. "What's new with you?"

Jordan waited, wondering what a good answer to that would be, and if Ellie really benefited from small talk at the moment, or if she was stalling.

"You know, whatever you need right now..."

"It's fine. Tell me what happened in those, what three days?"

"Well, let's see. I kind of stalked your ex and probably made her worry, so you might want to call her sometime soon."

"Rhonda?" Ellie scoffed. "I didn't think she'd care. If you have a current address, that's more than I have. Well, I could have looked it up. I didn't bother after she left me hanging with the rent, and the hair."

"Your hair is fine." At a red light, Jordan reached out to brush her fingers over the blonde strands. Ellie leaned into the touch.

Much of the time after Ellie had found her at Darby's had passed in a blur, and Jordan had little incentive to lift the shadows. She remembered, though, flinching at every touch, no matter how well meant. She should be relieved that Ellie was handling the situation so well, but these experiences could catch up with a person.

Then again, it depended on what exactly those experiences had been.

"At work everyone knows. I called Jack and Pauline. Kathryn knows because I was stupid enough to answer her call. On the bright side, maybe she'll stop bothering me for a while."

"She's bothering you, why? Shouldn't she be a little more grateful?"

They had arrived at the house, and Jordan walked around the car to open the door for Ellie. "Probably, but these aren't very humble people. She heard about you, so she probably won't stop calling." Jordan halted. "It's nothing, really." In comparison. She could tell from Ellie's expression that she got the meaning anyway.

"No, this is not how we're going to do this. I've got my notes, and I've got a pretty good memory. Not that there was so much to remember, mostly he brought me food, I tried to get away a few times and it finally worked. I got sick once because of the drugs, and I scraped my knees falling down those damn stairs. All in all not how I wanted to spend this week, but it could have been worse. Please believe me. I'll be okay, and I want to put this behind me as soon as possible. Doss and Waters got this. I would go for tea though."

Jordan laughed, surprised at the non-sequitur. "I'm afraid I don't have any, but I think there's some hot chocolate. Are you interested?"

"Why not? The guy wasn't going to let me starve, but he wasn't a big spender either, and I missed dinner at the hospital. Come to think of it, let's order in. No, don't say anything. I know your habits."

"All right. What would you like?"

"Whatever's fastest. I'll have the hot chocolate first."

Jordan wasn't surprised when Ellie wanted to turn in shortly after the meal. She didn't mind, grateful to make it an early night after the stress and fears of the past few days. She didn't expect Ellie to strip out of her nightgown and join her under the sheets naked, whispering, "I need to be close to you right now," but she had promised to go with whatever Ellie needed, and so be it.

❧

Danny wanted to drown his sorrow in a bottle of fine vodka, but as it was, he had to work, and no one cared about how he felt about this huge mess. Getting involved with Ward had been a mistake, but then again, it wasn't easy to find junkies he could have tricked into this scheme. Josh had seemed like the perfect candidate, doing any job for money...or the promise thereof. He was such an idiot, not playing by the rules and then getting himself killed.

What now?

At least he had taken some precautions, he thought, wiping the bar briskly, trying not to let anger get the better of him. He had to be extra careful now. He had rented the apartment in Josh's name, and that's where the cops would find the cell phone and every bit of evidence that tied him to the kidnapping.

They would look at Branson who got him the car, but so far, Danny was safe.

He wasn't only angry at Josh, but himself for being too chicken. There had been a small window from when he heard the gunshot to the police arriving on the scene, a time in which it could have been him to report the shot and possibly earn their gratitude.

He had wanted more, though, to be the hero who saved Ellie Harding from Ward. Then he would have gotten all the press and the attention. Eventually, the tightly knit group he watched at nights would understand he belonged with them, instead of scrubbing bars and washing glasses.

Neither Ellie nor Detective Carpenter was here tonight, probably still at the hospital. He watched Carpenter's partner come in with Officer McCarthy, the fiancé of the cop who got murdered not long ago. Danny frowned at their obvious body language, standing too close, whispering to each other.

If he was wearing the uniform, maybe women would be impressed with him too. He was so damn tired of being the one no one noticed. He would bet that most of the cops who frequented this place didn't even know his name. They knew his dad because he had been one of them. Danny was probably less than an afterthought to them.

"Can I have two Coronas?" the man asked. They didn't know him from any other waiter. A thought formed in Danny's mind, a new idea, something...

Bigger.

"Hello?"

"Yes. Sure. I'm sorry. Coming right up."

He couldn't carry it out right away, that would be too suspicious, but Danny had already proven that he could be cautious. With Josh dead and his associates unaware of Danny, he did have some leeway. Ward was the perfect scapegoat for the kidnapping.

This, the new idea, was so much better, and some of Josh's contacts could prove interesting for him.

Everyone would know his name eventually.

That made him feel better even though he could tell that Henderson—he knew all of their names—barely refrained from the impulse to roll his eyes.

Danny finally cut the lime, opened two bottles, and prepared them before he handed them to the detective.

Chapter Nine

T he first night after the unwelcome detour from their vacation passed without nightmares. Ellie knew from experience that she wasn't on the safe side yet, but she'd cherish small favors. Jordan hadn't asked, just held her until she fell asleep, and that had been so much better than spending the night at the hospital. That was a good thing about their relationship, she mused, slowly preparing herself for facing the day. They might deal differently, but they accepted each other's way.

Today, she'd meet with Detective Doss again, and then, thank God, things could go back to normal after they found the second guy. He wasn't a professional, but some guy acting out a fantasy—it shouldn't be that hard. She was still angry at him, at fate in general that proved to have such bad timing once more. They should be walking on the beach right now, not handling another curve ball thrown their way.

Ellie assumed she was lucky after all.

Everyone could stop worrying. If only they found him soon. She sat up, startling Jordan awake.

"You can stay a bit longer," she said, her voice still heavy with sleep. "I told Doss we meet her at eight. We stop for breakfast on the way."

"Let's get started. I really want to get this over with."

"I can imagine. Okay."

Half an hour later, they sat in the diner, Jordan with a barely touched toast and a black coffee. Ellie had ordered the brunch special and a café au lait. She might regret this later, but for now, she couldn't get enough of light, the freedom to move, and putting as much food on her plate as she damn well pleased.

She saw Jordan regard her with affection and barely concealed amusement.

"You're going to eat all of that?"

"Well, I'd rather ruin my figure with cocktails under palm trees, but since that wasn't an option..."

Jordan took her hand on the table. "We'll get back to that. I promise."

"I know. In the meantime, there are ways to stay in shape...by which I mean you can take me to your gym sometime." Ellie laughed at Jordan's self-conscious expression. "No, I didn't mean that, actually. You got it right the first time."

"Funny. Let's wrap this up...If we're lucky, we can reschedule vacation time before we see Doss, and I'll drive you home after."

"What, why?"

"You didn't think you were going back to work today? Come on. Give it a few days. The doctor might have been okay with you going home, but I didn't hear anything about work."

Everything Jordan said sounded logical and sensible, yet it left Ellie with an uneasy feeling. She wasn't prepared for any of this, sitting at home alone, in the apartment she'd wanted to leave for months, that had been invaded by two criminals, their degrees of insanity and ruthlessness varying. This wasn't a good time. She wanted out.

Maybe she had imagined this all along, approaching the subject carefully during the vacation...Then again, it might not be the best idea. Jordan wasn't ready. They'd only been dating for a short time and after her tumultuous relationship with her ex, moving in together was probably the last thing on her mind.

Bad timing. They were pretty good at it.

"Just until the weekend, to make sure you're okay to run after bad guys again," Jordan said softly.

Perhaps Ellie should simply ask her. She waited too long, and the moment passed, the waitress stopping by their table to bring the bill. Jordan picked it up, but Ellie snatched it out of her hand.

"No way. That wouldn't be fair."

Jordan hesitated but didn't try to stop her.

✦

"He was...odd, to say the least. Not impulsively violent. He must have been planning for a while, and that's why I'm sure there was another guy. Ward only came in later, and I recognized his voice. From that other time." Ellie saw Doss and Jordan exchange a look. She had handed over her notes from the hospital with as much detail as her mind could produce and tried to sound calm and professional. They had no reason to doubt her perception—she wasn't just any kidnap victim, she was a police officer, and for most of the time, she had been awake and aware. Her life hadn't been threatened except for that one time and...Ward was dead. She didn't have to think about him anymore.

"Anyway, this guy didn't even flinch when I threw food at him, just went to get a rag and a brush to clean it up. He only drugged me after I'd hit him in the face. He almost reminded me of that case, I'm sure you looked into that, those brothers. They weren't violent per se but wanted to get back at the other guy. This one was different, I believe he didn't choose me randomly. After all, the jerk knew I was supposed to go on a vacation. It didn't seem...sexual." Ellie sensed that the two women listening to her almost felt the same kind of relief at this assessment. Ward hadn't been that harmless. Ward was dead. She couldn't repeat it often enough in her mind.

"Ellie, we've turned the apartment upside down," Maria Doss said, her expression serious. "It was rented in Ward's name. The computer belonged to him as well. We found the cell phone he used to send you texts from, a file on you, information about your schedule, what you were doing after work, et cetera. Photos. They're still processing the prints, but so far, we haven't found any proof that there was even another person in there other than you and Ward."

"No, that's not possible." Ellie shook her head, vehemently, to underline her protest. "He's still out there. He might not have been violent this time, but what if he tries again? It might not even be me, and at some point, he could snap. We've got to keep looking."

"We checked Mercer's alibi," Jordan said. "What about Branson?" she asked Maria. "I can't believe this guy keeps slipping through our fingers."

"We can't tie him to this case," Maria answered. "He admitted providing the car for Ward, that's all. He wasn't supposed to ask any questions, and he didn't."

"I don't believe that," Jordan said.

"I don't know what he knew, but he wasn't the other guy in the apartment." Ellie remembered Tucker Branson, his voice, the threats he made in court. One of her first arrests, she had felt proud when the case came to court, not so much after he screamed about how much she'd regret it. She didn't want to imagine how he would have reacted, had she thrown eggs and coffee at him. "He's violent. If it had been him, I might not be sitting here. You have the car, don't you? The guy has to have taken off those damn gloves at some point. He made eggs one time. You looked at Ward's rap sheet? He didn't care whether I had anything to eat or not."

"Okay. As soon as we find something, you'll be the first to know."

"Believe me, there was someone else, and it was not Branson. I know that guy. He gave me a pretty good scare back then."

"We will find him," Jordan said, but all of a sudden, Ellie wasn't so sure.

It wasn't fair. After finally identifying the perp who had attacked her months ago and almost did it again in the mystery man's apartment, she should have some peace.

"Excuse me," she said, "is this all? I would like to talk to Kate for a moment."

"Yes, sure. We'll keep you informed."

Ellie couldn't make much sense of the look Maria cast at Kate standing on the other side of the room with Henderson. She wanted to exchange a few words with her friend, make sure she knew everything was okay.

During the few seconds it took her to walk over to them, Kate and Derek had ended their conversation, and he greeted Ellie briefly before heading to his desk, where he picked up a file and left.

Kate embraced her. "I'm so happy to see you here. You're coming back to work already?"

"Tomorrow," Ellie said, determined. "Friday at the latest, depending on how soon I can clear it with the doctor. Hell, I'm a little banged up from falling down a few steps. I don't need to sit at home, especially when the guy is still out there." She saw Kate's eyes widen. "Not Ward, obviously. There was someone else."

"Are you sure? I mean…I'm willing to admit, I'd be scared out of my mind."

It wasn't something Ellie wanted to hear. "You do what you have to do, there's not much else to it. I'm really sorry," she hurried to add. "It's nothing in comparison."

Kate sighed. "Take good care of yourself, okay? I'd really like to talk sometime soon. Maybe we could hang out for a bit on the weekend?"

"I could meet you later tonight. We might be at the *Code 7*."

"Really? Shouldn't you...?"

"Like I said, I'll clear it with the doctor. I'm fine." Kate looked doubtful, but she didn't protest. "Find me that guy. Then I'll be even better."

Ellie spent the rest of the day keeping busy, longer than she'd hoped at the doctor's office—hers was no emergency after all, only in her eyes, it was. She had seen the doubt in her colleagues' eyes, and she would have none of that.

She could see him clearly in her mind, the dark clothes, the mask, hear his pathetic attempt at altering his voice, then faltering. Not Ward.

She went back to the moment she'd come out of the bathroom, slamming her cuffed hands in his face. That must have hurt. He must have some marks, and she'd written it down in the notes and told Doss. Ward's face had sported the gash from the tab, but nothing else.

That man wasn't a ghost, he had to be in hiding somewhere—and he'd been clever enough to rent the apartment for the purpose of her abduction in Ward's name.

To her chagrin, her doctor insisted on at least another couple of sick days, and she still had to schedule an appointment with the department shrink.

Ellie was frustrated and offended by the red tape that kept her from carrying on with her life. After all, it was nothing like getting on the radar of a serial killer. Jordan still had a lot on her plate, dealing with the aftermath of that case, the revelations about her birthparents, and the way her relationship with Bethany ended.

Right—this wasn't such a good moment to ask if Ellie could move in, because she hated her apartment. She'd be patient. It had paid off before.

She made a call to both Jordan and Kate, telling them to meet her at the bar later.

Just a few more days. And maybe a few more nights would convince Jordan that they were compatible in close quarters as well.

∞

On the bright side, Ellie had managed to avoid the apartment for most of the day. With a sigh, she unlocked the door and stepped inside, taking a few deep breaths. It was over. She wouldn't break down crying. All she wanted for the moment was to get some clothes, go take a shower at Jordan's house and chase the memories from her mind, spend an evening among friends.

Friends who had been through worse. She still wondered what Kate's cryptic words might have meant, but she felt too tired and dispirited herself to try and solve the mystery. Kate would tell her later.

She grabbed a few clothes from the closet, underwear, a couple pairs of shoes, halting halfway through her actions. She hoped Jordan wouldn't misinterpret the fact that Ellie simply needed a little time away from this place so she could eventually come back, clean it up and do the best she could to get the hell out of here. It was only normal. She'd never liked it so much to begin with. Who could blame her if it didn't feel safe to her any longer?

Ellie was glad when she closed the door behind her once again. She took the elevator down to the lobby and left the building, halting abruptly halfway to her car. A drop of sweat was sneaking down her spine as she tried to shake the feeling of being watched. She turned into all directions, but there was only the neighbor from across the street, pushing her baby in a stroller. She waved.

Hesitantly, Ellie raised her hand, waving back. She turned to look back at the building but couldn't detect anyone lurking behind windows.

So she was a bit overly careful—perfectly normal. It would go away with time.

Kate was already there when she walked through the door of the *Code 7*. Ellie took a deep breath, relieved to be back in a space that had only ever been associated with mostly good experiences, friends, laughter, coming together to grieve with people she could trust. And, let's not forget, the incredibly hot encounter in the bathroom stall that no one but Ellie and Jordan should ever know about.

She could feel her body relax, and the crazy past days fell away as if they were nothing but a bad dream. That's how Ellie would treat it. All else wouldn't serve her. She ordered a beer at the bar and then went to join her friend who looked like she hadn't slept in days.

When would she be able to stop reassuring people that everything was fine?

"Hey," Ellie said and took a seat across from her. Jordan wasn't there yet. "What did you want to talk about?"

Kate shrugged. "Everything and nothing. I'm not sure I should bother you with this. You've been through a horrible time."

"Oh, come on." Ellie laughed a little, noticing Kate's uncomfortable demeanor. "It was boring and annoying for most of the time, and it certainly screwed up my vacation plans. Horrible...I think some of us have been through horrible things, but those were petty, small-time criminals. I just hope we'll have the other one behind bars soon."

"You are certain that there was someone else," Kate observed. "I hear there's no proof of anyone other than Ward?"

"They're going to find proof, I am sure. Now, let's talk about you, okay?"

"I'm afraid there isn't much to say you don't already know. I was worried sick about you. Jensen...I miss him..." She choked up at that, making Ellie think she'd been right about assuming she wasn't the one who had it worst. No innocent people had died in the course of her abduction. As for Ward, she couldn't muster much sympathy for him. She'd run into bad luck, which, in Ellie's opinion, was a far cry from Kate's situation. Or Jordan's.

"Oh Ellie, I screwed up. Badly."

"No. You did nothing wrong. You couldn't have..."

"Hey there! Ellie, I didn't expect you here tonight, but it's great to see you," Libby Marshall greeted her. She was accompanied by another officer she'd been dating for some time, and shortly after him, Jordan entered the bar.

Ellie cast Kate a quick look. "It's okay," Kate said, though her smile looked a bit forced. "Go."

"Are you sure?"

"Positive. I assume Libby and Matt will keep me company."

"That's the plan," Libby confirmed, taking a seat on a barstool. "Good to have you back, Ellie."

"It's good to be back. See you later."

Jordan hugged her in greeting. It was a relief to be able to stay in her embrace for a moment and not have to worry about who knew. No more hiding. She caught the guy behind the bar regarding them thoughtfully, or maybe he was staring into nothing. The owner's son. He helped out with the bar, but hardly ever talked to patrons except taking their orders.

Ellie and Jordan found a table.

"I've been waiting for Doss's call, but nothing to far. Is there anything new?"

"I'm afraid not," Jordan said.

"What does that mean? Is it her theory that I wasn't thinking clearly? Or yours?" That would be infinitely worse. If Doss thought Ellie had made up the second man because of stress, it wasn't good either.

Jordan raised her hands. "Relax, it's not what I believe. It's entirely possible that someone set up Ward to be the main suspect. We're looking into Ward's connections, but no such luck so far. He used to have money but didn't for many years. The people he hung out with don't rent in that neighborhood."

"So, the other guy, he has a bit of money available, a plan, and he needs a scapegoat. How does he find Ward? Someone's not only been watching me, but they might have been aware of cases I worked. How is that possible? There are only certain people who have access to that information or could easily get it."

"You're not saying what I think you're saying."

Ellie shrugged, frustrated with the lack of progress. The man in the apartment hadn't struck her as extraordinarily intelligent, someone who could escape the police for a long time. It was impossible that he had left no traces.

"I don't know. Maybe. It does make sense though."

"What about Rhonda? Did you know she had an ex hanging around? A guy?"

"Okay, that's news to me like most things about Rhonda, but then again, she just disappeared on me. I don't think she ever wasted a thought on wanting me back." Thinking about Rhonda brought back her present dilemma immediately. "I hope you don't mind I invited myself to your place for a few days...You know I still have to clean up my apartment, and after that I want to look for something new. Actually, I wanted to do that months ago, so now's the time."

Ellie held her breath. *Ball's in your court.* All the clichés she'd ever heard about lesbians moving in together too soon floated through her mind. There was of course Jordan's very specific situation, the recent ending of a long-term relationship, and the fact that she valued her own space so highly. Ellie was aware of how much they differed in this regard. Hell, the apartment had felt big even when Rhonda still lived there.

"It's okay. You can come stay with me for a while, until you find something new," Jordan said, her smile belying the hint of nervousness. "I haven't changed much since I moved in, but you know there's enough space."

Space, it was always an issue with Jordan. She was entitled, Ellie reminded herself.

"You don't mind if I sleep naked in your bed again?"

"I don't mind at all."

"Good. Maybe sleep isn't all we'll do. Now I'd really like a glass of wine."

Jordan was quick to get up and get it for her.

⚜

Five minutes later Jordan was almost grateful the guy behind the bar was such a klutz, getting wine all over her shirt instead of in the glass—she still wasn't sure how he had managed that. In any case, it gave her a small reprieve and time to calm down.

This was how it had happened with Bethany, a tough case, a few drinks after work, a few dates and the next moment, a moving company was involved, and they signed the lease on a condo. It had taken her nine years to get out.

The present situation was completely different, of course. She didn't blame Ellie for wanting to finally get out of a place that carried many bad memories, especially since one of them was associated with Jonathan Darby. She knew Ellie was more aware than anyone else in her life of what significance buying her own space, living on her own for the first time in a long time, had for Jordan.

She loved Ellie. She wanted a future with her. Jordan had hoped that future would include separate living spaces for a little while longer, and somehow it made her feel like she'd done something wrong. A vacation together had seemed like a much more logical and safer step.

She couldn't mess this up, not like she had with Bethany. No pressure.

Eventually, she stopped rubbing at the stain and decided the tank top she wore underneath was decent enough for the *Code 7*. She had promised Ellie her wine, time to get back in there.

When she returned, Ellie was still sitting in the same space, waiting patiently. Maybe Jordan had overreacted. Ellie could be impulsive, and Jordan loved that about her, but she was also one of the people who had been most patient with Jordan in the past few weeks, months, when everything seemed to be falling apart.

They'd be all right.

Her cell phone rang when she finally put the glass in front of Ellie, and seeing who the caller was, Jordan sighed and excused herself.

"Darla. What's the matter?"

The young woman had been her CI for the past couple of years. The latest case involving Jordan's biological father TJ Pratt bore a great risk for her, and Jordan had promised to put her in touch with people who could help her make some changes in her life. She hadn't heard from Darla since.

"Can we talk?"

"Can it wait until tomorrow? Is everything all right with the program?"

The last thing Jordan knew was that she had gone back to school and taken a cashier job in a supermarket.

"Yeah, I'm doing all right," Darla said. "It's not about that. I...I really need to talk, but tomorrow is fine."

"Sure?"

"Yes, I swear."

"Okay. I'll meet you after my shift, in the usual place."

"You're still going to pay?" Darla asked, laughing, but she sounded wistful.

"Of course. See you then."

"I was kidding. You don't have to do that anymore. I look forward to seeing you. Bye."

"Is she all right?"

Ellie had met Darla, in fact saved her from a ruthless criminal who had associated himself with Pratt. No, there was no reason to cozy up to Kathryn anytime soon after the many harmful decisions she'd made, including her brief affair with Pratt.

"I think so. She wants to talk. I'll see her tomorrow. I think she stayed pretty much on track."

Ellie shuddered, no doubt thinking about the moment they had found her.

"After what she's been through, I'd be surprised if she didn't. She really wanted to make this chance count. You know, you could have gone now."

"I know, but it didn't sound urgent...and I really want to spend time with you."

"I like that," Ellie said. "And don't worry, I'm pretty easy to live with."

Pretty easy to love, too.

His plans were slowly taking shape, and so Danny started to feel better about himself again, less angry, when he saw them at the bar, acting as if nothing had happened, as if his actions didn't have any weight.

He could imagine what they thought: couldn't cut it as a cop, couldn't even make it as a criminal. It was all Ward's fault. He had freaked her out. If he'd managed to get Ellie Harding to the new location and then be the savior, everything would have gone according to plan. The first plan.

Danny could see that it might have been a mistake on his part to focus solely on Harding. His new considerations were bigger and would make him look even better in the aftermath. This was his last chance at something big...and he would take it. At the same time, he could get rid of something he'd hated for so long.

Between serving drinks and counting change, he observed the people sitting together in groups, laughing, chatting, some in serious conversation. He envied the invisible threads between them, the common goal, and the way they pulled together when a life was on the line. He was just as good as any of them.

He would prove it.

Soon.

Chapter Ten

She didn't say it nearly often enough, but Jordan admired Ellie greatly. Maybe she'd had a head start earlier in life, with decent parents and an overall nourishing social environment, but there was no doubt she handled life's blows differently. Her stubborn optimistic outlook intrigued Jordan to no end, even though she was torn at the moment, with Ellie naked in her arms, her kiss demanding.

No one put an experience like that behind them so quickly—but maybe it wasn't about that. If this was what Ellie needed, right now, Jordan was more than willing to comply.

"I'm not fragile," Ellie whispered, "and I want you as much as I did last week."

Jordan wasn't in a position to argue much when Ellie undid the clasp of her bra, tossing the garment aside, and her fingers slid beneath the hem of her panties.

"Wow. Are you sure?"

"I think this would be cruel of me if I wasn't. Don't think about it for a moment, please? If we were in a hotel room in Costa Rica right now, this is exactly what we'd be doing. I refuse to give him that much power. This is what I want."

Jordan gasped at the warm pressure of her wandering fingertips.

"I'm pretty sure you want it too," Ellie concluded, a smile in her voice.

"Believe me, I do, but we've got time. Slow down for a bit, okay?"

Ellie smiled. "Whatever you like. I'm all yours."

Sometimes, it was hard to believe, but Jordan was determined to make sure Ellie wouldn't regret her decision, ever. She kissed her softly, lowering her body over hers, careful to avoid her bruised knees. Jordan wasn't at all sure that this was the answer to all the open questions, but it seemed like the best available for now, and they had certainly earned this moment out of time. It was a better way to look at it than wondering if they had done something so unforgivable that bad luck would follow them from now on. She lost herself in the sensations, Ellie's warm skin under her hands, her gasp turning into moans. It was almost too quick when she shivered against Jordan, her hands gripping the sheet in a tight grip. Then again, everything had happened quickly between them, and the U-Haul might not be too far in the future.

Jordan sat up, trying to get her bearings, and understand what had happened the past few days—or since the day she had decided that she could no longer pretend she and Bethany could have a future together.

Ellie embraced her from behind. "Don't worry. You know I'm a bit strange sometimes, and I don't expect you to under-stand all of it, but there's something you should know. I wanted you long before all the bad stuff happened. Well, maybe not long, but before. I wouldn't have slept with just anyone."

"I know. I'm sorry."

"You don't have to be. That's why I'm telling you." Her hands skimmed over Jordan's ribs, wandering higher to cup her breasts. "It's not just about me though. I know that compared to what you've been through, I…"

"It's not a competition. Ellie...Would you mind if we just went to sleep? It's going to be a long day tomorrow."

"Not a competition. I get it." Ellie smiled, but her disappointment came through anyway. "I understand, it's still early. It's just that I don't want them to take any more out of my life, out of our lives. They don't deserve that much power, you know? Are you sure it's about that?"

It had been days since Ellie escaped from her kidnapper. What else would it be? That was a can of worms better left unopened. It had been too easy to lay part of the blame on Bethany because she kept pushing. If Jordan let too much of her past interfere with a relationship with someone she loved, it would be all her fault.

"I want you to take the time you need to work through what happened, that's all."

Ellie pulled the cover up high and lay back down. "I'm sure you hated it when someone said that to you. It's...what it is. People are different, and it helps me more than anything that you're not treating me like I'm about to shatter into a million pieces. I am not."

"I'm glad to hear that," Jordan whispered, pulling her close after she'd turned off the light.

Part of her envied Ellie for always looking ahead, and maybe she hoped that she might be able to adopt some of it someday.

⌒⌒

Jordan's reaction had given Ellie a lot to think about that night, yet she was up early to make breakfast, trying to figure out the pieces in her mind. She hoped she had assured Jordan enough, or that this was even the strategy she needed to follow. She didn't doubt Jordan's commitment to her for a moment. There was no doubt they had considerable odds stacked against them.

Ellie, however, was used to getting what she wanted, even if that included difficult and at times, painful, detours. Her career was on track, and she was with the woman she'd wanted in her life more than anything. So far, so good. She had to tread carefully. Too much had happened in a short amount of time, too many revelations.

In spite of being determined to make it an early day, Jordan didn't seem eager to get it started when she came out of the bedroom, her hair still wet from the shower.

"Thank you." She sighed. "This looks great. I'm sorry I was such a downer last night. I didn't mean to...I'm glad you're here."

Here in this place, or here as in alive and well? Ellie didn't want to dwell on semantics right now.

"I have no reason to complain, but I guess I owe you. Feel free to collect anytime soon."

Jordan couldn't suppress the smile. "I'll remember that."

"Did you sleep okay?"

"Shouldn't I be asking you that?"

"It's not a competition, remember?" Ellie sat down across from Jordan after she'd poured coffee for the two of them. "I'm not...panicking. I'm mad at how all this went down, and apparently, there's still no lead on the other guy. No message from Doss. Libby and Kate would call me too if there was anything to go on. Speaking of which, I should probably see Kate. She was acting strange last night. I know she's still grieving, but this was different. What do you think?"

"I slept okay," Jordan said too quickly.

Ellie had seen her in the interrogation room, but the private persona of Jordan Carpenter was someone entirely different. She couldn't lie to save her life. Okay, that was a bad metaphor. They had both done what they needed to do under most dangerous circumstances. "You know something I don't. Is she in trouble?"

"Not exactly, but I imagine she's feeling bad." Jordan hesitated for a moment. "It appears that she's seeing Derek."

Ellie could feel her eyes grow wide. This was not what she'd expected. Somewhere in the back of her mind, she felt elated that Jordan would tell her, testimony how they'd gotten close over a short time. Well, maybe part of it was Ellie's own interrogation tactic. She'd make a good detective, soon.

"Wow. I mean, why? This is sudden."

"I told Derek my opinion. He was not amused. I'm not sure what happened there."

Now Kate's cryptic words made sense. Ellie was grateful she wouldn't walk into her next conversation with her friend and get blindsided.

"I guess we can't blame them," she offered.

Jordan shook her head. "That's not the same."

They weren't cheating on anyone, Ellie almost said, but she held back the words, thinking this subject might be a little too complicated at the moment. She was surprised but didn't think Kate should beat herself up over seeking comfort and solace in being with someone, even if it didn't last.

"I'll call her," she said. "I hope that when you come back from work, you'll bring me some good news about our phantom."

⸎

Jordan, like her colleagues, proved to be unable to fulfill Ellie's wish—the second man in the apartment where she'd been held remained a mystery. She was equally unsuccessful trying to talk to Derek who was still avoiding her. The moment she walked up to his desk, his phone rang, and he held up a hand. Jordan stayed in the vicinity, seeing his expression turn from mildly annoyed to serious.

Immediately, her thoughts went to Ellie. Derek hung up, hesitating for a split second.

"I need to get this to the lieutenant right away. You might want to join me."

"Bad news?"

"You could say that. We're getting some unwanted company for the holiday. Let's hope we can contain this before someone gets killed."

"That sounds bad."

"Because it is." He knocked on the lieutenant's office door, and their superior called them in where Derek detailed the tip he had gotten a tip from a CI. Apparently, someone had been asking around about explosives, and arranged a meeting with somebody who could provide them. The items on the priority list shifted again. Rumor had it there was a seller coming to town with access to alarming quantities, and the name of a wanted suspect came up: Troy Haynes who had allegedly been involved in black market explosives deals. There was concern he might be moving up in the game, associating with individuals and groups more dangerous than the occasional corrupt businessman.

"I'll make some calls right now," the lieutenant said. "Let's see what our friends from the Bureau can give us on Haynes. They'll send someone."

Especially with the holiday coming, no one wanted to take the risk that the man who had made those inquiries, could succeed.

Within the next hour, a joint task force was set up with the FBI, including Agent Russo whom they'd met through Bethany, Derek and Jordan.

"We've been after this guy for a while," Russo said. "Thanks to Detective Henderson's informant, we now have a possible location."

"Haynes will be in town this week, possibly as soon as the day after tomorrow." Derek explained. "That means someone already asked for his services, and we want that guy, as well as Haynes' boss."

"Why is Homicide in this?" Jordan asked. "There are other open cases that—"

"Because we're hoping to prevent multiple homicides here."

"Okay. I get that." She shrugged, feeling unfairly scolded by her partner who was obviously still mad at her. "Did Haynes' deals ever get anyone killed before? Why do we think it might this time?"

"My guy says the buyer is planning, I quote, 'something big.' That should be enough to have all of us worried."

"Yes, I agree."

Russo spoke up again. "There'll be 24/7 surveillance." He pointed to the map showing the abandoned house the informant had identified. "Detective, I want you to keep close contact with your CI, make sure we know if anything changes, or if he knows more, time, location, anything. We don't want to take any chances."

Derek nodded.

A somber group disassembled, and Jordan found herself looking at a few uncomfortable nights in close quarters with Derek—unless their suspects showed up tonight, which would be a preferable outcome. She called Darla and asked to reschedule their meeting. At least, Darla didn't seem to mind.

Night after night, they kept watching the building that was supposed to be the scene of the deal, once a two-family home, now housing mostly spiders and bats.

After night four with none of those criminals turning up, and the communication between them still reduced to the bare necessities, Jordan decided it was time to move on. She was still certain she had been right, after all. Derek's affair with Mc-Carthy wasn't the smartest move, but they were both adults. It was none of her business. Perhaps, she had secretly been worried about Ellie's reaction, but she didn't seem to mind much.

In fact, Ellie's only problem appeared to be that they never got the chance to go on their vacation. She was determined to get back to work as soon as possible and get some hours in so they could reschedule soon.

"So...are you ever going to talk to me again?"

"I talked to you when I asked you if we still had coffee."

Jordan leaned back into her seat and stared out into the darkness. "Maybe I owe you an apology. Frankly, I don't know. What the hell were you thinking? It might not be up for me to judge, but I'm still curious. Everyone seems to want to compare this situation to me and Ellie. It's not the same. We both made that choice, and we're doing our best to make it work."

"What makes you think Kate and I aren't?"

"We're not exactly proud. Those were your words."

"It's not the best timing, but I'm serious about her. That's all you need to know."

"And Maria?"

Derek shook his head, laughing. "That's it. Why don't we analyze your life for a change?"

Jordan shrugged. "Too many have tried and failed? You're right. I assume you know what you're doing."

"How's Ellie?" he asked.

"She seems fine. She's back to normal work hours, staying with me for a while."

"I've heard. A while, or is it..."

"Maybe. For now, she doesn't really feel like going back there, but she's going to look for another place sometime soon."

Derek's gaze said that he wasn't too sure about that. Jordan wasn't either, and she hated how that made her feel anxious. A little sooner or later, it shouldn't make a difference, should it?

She jumped at the sound alerting her to a new text message.

I haven't heard from you in days. Are you OK?

Jordan shook her head at the screen. "I might have to file a restraining order against Kathryn. She doesn't stop calling and texting, and I have no desire to see her again."

"Sounds like you could have used that vacation."

"Oh yes. That's another thing we're working on. I'd feel better if we could find that second guy first."

"You believe he actually exists?"

The question surprised Jordan. She had expected the mysterious guy trying to buy explosives to take precedence, but for all she knew, they were still looking for a second kidnapper.

"Maria's not talking to me all that much, for obvious reasons, but I overheard Bristol. There's only evidence to put Ward in that room, and he's dead. Branson got him the car, but apparently, that's all he did. Ward's fingerprints are all over this—it makes sense to assume he was working on his own."

"Yeah, maybe," Jordan had to admit. Ellie wouldn't be happy with this solution, but it made sense—if Ward had tried to trick her earlier by altering his voice, he might even go as far as making her think there was more than one kidnapper. It didn't mean she couldn't trust her perception ever again. It was hard to keep a clear mind when being held against your will, with a captor whose demeanor could take a turn for the worse any time.

But Ellie hadn't sounded like her mind was clouded by stress and fear. In fact, she was adamant about having heard the second person. Jordan would believe her unless proven otherwise. For all they knew, Ward made a perfect scapegoat for the other guy.

"All right, it's good we cleared all that up before he arrived," she said with regard to the shadowy figure materializing out of the bushes, shoulders hunched against the rain. The entrance they were watching was the only access to the house. Whatever the person hoped to find there, the people he wanted to talk to hadn't arrived yet.

Minutes passed by, ten, then twenty.

"Do you think someone tipped them off?" Jordan wondered out loud.

"No. Mac would have told me."

He couldn't get out anywhere other than the front door, so they were going to wait, and if no one joined him, invite him to a conversation.

However, after another fifteen minutes, a van pulled up in front of the house.

"It's getting interesting," Derek remarked when two men emerged, carrying a case each.

"Yeah. We should join the party." They got out of the car and carefully advanced towards the front door. Within minutes, other members of the task force had joined them.

None of the men were one of the first floor as far as they could see, but there was a faint light upstairs. Flashlights.

They went back to the front door, and Jordan opened it carefully, stepping inside. Derek followed her. They could hear muted voices from upstairs. Wooden steps led to the upper floor, the railing continuing into a gallery upstairs. Since those men had nowhere to go, it was better to greet them at the entrance. They waited for a tense two, three minutes until there was movement from above. Jordan prepared herself for confrontation as more officers approached from the back. They should be able to wrap this up quickly.

The men who had carried whatever in those cases didn't look like they'd be interested in a friendly chat. There were shouts, something about the price of the merchandise, and then a gunshot upstairs.

Crap.

Exchanging a quick signal, they sprinted up the wooden stairs, training their weapons on the two men who didn't even see them coming until they yelled at them.

"Police! Drop your weapons!"

"Fuck!" One of them complied, his expression between anger and disbelief as he turned away from the open window where the apparent buyer who had met them had jumped.

The other one had a cool calculating look on his face, Jordan noticed as she kept her gun trained on him.

"Don't try anything," she warned. His finger twitched slightly on the weapon, but then he laid it down and Derek put the cuffs on him.

Jordan alerted their colleagues downstairs to the jumper. If they were lucky, they'd catch him running away from the scene.

⁂

It turned out they weren't that lucky. Troy Haynes, one of the two arrests, had a long record. He'd been selling guns and drugs on and off and was more than happy to turn on his partner who was in the bigger game, dealing with anything that could blow up, selling it to anyone who was interested. Haynes described the buyer as some "scrawny kid" who looked like he'd be "pissing his pants if he had to light some fireworks" but brought the money anyway. Not that anyone had any money now, because he'd thrown it out the window and jumped after it. "Kid had balls after all," Haynes commented. How could he have gotten away with the building surrounded?

"Was he the one who contacted you first?"

Jordan thought it was a terrifying world in which some scrawny kid could hook up with dealers like that and get enough C4 to blow out a couple of buildings at the very least, if he cared to. He got away with some of it.

"I don't know anything about that. I just came to get the money."

"Sure you did. The scrawny kid, did he talk about what he needed those explosives for?"

"Not a word, but I told you before, I didn't even know what was inside until they opened the cases. Kid didn't talk much. He looked freaked out pretty much the whole time. Wait a minute. I think they were talking about an order from a guy named Watts? That's all I remember. Am I going to get my deal or what? I told you everything I know."

"We'll see about that. How about we take a break, and we see if you remember some more?"

Jordan stepped outside the interrogation area, coming face to face with her superior.

"Sir. Anything on the runner?"

"No, and Henderson's not having any luck with the other guy. It's a good thing though you got to them when you did. This is odd. It's not that easy to get in touch with these people."

"Yes, I wonder how he did it, even with one go between contact. The way they describe him he's not one of the regulars. Let's hope he doesn't find anyone else to do business with," Jordan said. "On the other hand, he could just go on the Internet and find his material there."

"You're not helping, Carpenter."

"Sorry about that," she mumbled. It was a valid question though. The Internet was the first place to go for many criminals these days—often, they didn't have to resort to deals like this that left them out in the open, visible. "We'll keep an eye on purchases in the area anyway, online and in person. He's already gone this far, he might want to try again. Not that I trust him so much," she gestured to Haynes on the other side of the two-way mirror, "but it worries me that we might be dealing with an angry guy buying C4. Whatever his plans are, they can't be any good."

"Right. That's why you're going to find him before he can realize them."

"Yes, sir."

Ellie was still home when Jordan returned at the end of her shift, but in uniform, coffee ready.

"Good morning," she greeted her. "Would you like to eat something...or straight to bed?"

Jordan almost laughed at the possible insinuations. Every once in a while, when they met like this in the morning, neither sleep nor food was the first thing that happened. She assumed Ellie didn't have that much time though, and Jordan had trouble deciding whether hunger or the need to sleep was stronger.

"Coffee first, thanks. I won't be hanging out nights with Derek for a while either."

"You caught the guy?"

"Not the guy, unfortunately, but two fellows who were to sell two cases of C4 to him. We have all kinds of prints, but that probably won't help."

"Sorry about that. Would you like eggs? I made some. Don't worry, I can clean up before I go," Ellie added quickly.

"It's fine. And yes, I think I'll have some, thank you."

It would all work out fine. Even with conflicting schedules, they were already managing to maintain some sort of routine.

Jordan had to admit it was a relief having Ellie around, after everything, and realizing this house had enough space for the two of them. Maybe the amount of space hadn't been the problem to begin with, between her and Bethany. The fact that it had been filled with suspicion and resentment had made it seem more claustrophobic. Between her and Ellie, the air was clear and mostly calm. It was a refreshing, new feeling. Jordan reminded herself to look at rescheduling the trip soon. Next it occurred to her that she didn't even know when Ellie's birthday was...but that was something she could easily check at work. Later.

Chapter Eleven

There were still some loose ends to tie up. Since returning to work, Ellie had spent as long as she could without raising suspicion looking at mug shots and listening to interrogation tapes in similar cases, with no success. She agreed that Tucker Branson hadn't changed his ways much, but he hadn't been the man with the mask, his build and demeanor all wrong. Now everyone was most concerned with the buyer of the C4 and keeping the holiday celebrations safe.

Sometimes, the sound of a door being locked made her flinch, still. That wasn't so bad all in all, but it wasn't good enough for Ellie. She wanted closure, a clean slate. Now that they could finally be together, she didn't want any distraction. The job. The relationship. She'd never gone that far off track before, and she needed to get back to the plan as soon as possible.

"Officer Harding?"

The soft-spoken address made her look up, and the next moment, Ellie did a double-take. She hadn't seen Darla Pierson since she'd been admitted to the hospital after a vicious beating. Now, the visible marks were gone, but that wasn't the only change. Jordan had helped her former informant to go back to school and find a job.

"Ms. Pierson, how are you?"

"I'm okay. Do you know if Jordan is here? I need to talk to her."

"She'll come in later today, but I assume she called you back? The last days were pretty hectic."

"Yeah, I know. We rescheduled, but I was hoping to meet her here."

"Can I take a message?"

Ellie blushed as it was so obvious what Darla needed to tell Jordan. She scolded herself for her initial, prejudiced notion. For all she knew, Darla had everything under control and was checking in to say hello, or maybe thank you. The fact that she was expecting didn't have to mean she was in trouble.

"I can come by later," Darla offered with a smile that seemed forced.

"I could call her if you like."

"No, thanks. Have a good day."

Ellie watched her walk away, wondering if she should warn Jordan. Neither of them should assume anything beyond the obvious facts.

She went back to her reading, minimizing the screen quickly when she saw Sergeant Bristol approaching her desk.

"Harding, you're here, good. I want you to meet McCarthy and Marshall at the stadium. There's some fight about tickets for tomorrow's holiday event. Apparently, they're all sold out already, and some customers didn't take it so well."

"Wow, really? Okay. I'll be on my way."

Ellie found it baffling that people spent this much money to watch fireworks, not to mention the money they did spend on actual fireworks.

When she arrived on the scene, there were already two squad cars next to the ticket booth, one man in handcuffs glaring at another who was holding some cloth against his bleeding nose.

Two more were in handcuffs, a man and a woman, shouting obscenities at each other until Kate yelled, "Hey! That's enough!"

Kate had toughened up since the horrific incidents that led to her fiancé's death, they all had.

Libby Marshall came over to Ellie.

"Hey, good you're here. You may drive some of these charming folks to the station. Wow, getting into a fistfight over a place to watch fireworks? Okay. The lady and the gentleman over there are the least likely to try and kill each other during the ride, so I'm leaving them to you."

"Did they come here together?"

"No." Libby laughed. "Don't ask. Will we see you later?"

"I'm not sure, but maybe I'll make it for one beer."

Libby's expression had turned serious. "Please do. Kate could use some show of support. You probably have an idea why. Don't look so surprised." Libby sighed. "Someone always finds out, and a couple of guys have been jerks about it. Not that they would say anything to Henderson. You know how it is."

"Yeah. I wish the people we work with knew better."

"Don't we all. Anyway, it would be nice if you could come by."

Ellie delivered her drunk and disorderly charges for booking, wondering what the same people had said about her and Jordan. The downside of a tightly knit community was that it was hard to keep secrets. She didn't know the whole story, and it seemed that neither did Jordan, but she didn't think it was fair to shame Kate for being human. She would say so to anyone who'd bother to ask her opinion.

She didn't get to talk to Jordan all day, and when she returned home after work, Jordan's car wasn't in her parking spot yet. Ellie wondered if she had an opportunity to talk to Darla, and what the real story was here. Either way, Jordan had gone out of her way to help her, and there was no way either of them could control the outcome. Ellie realized that for the first time in hours, she hadn't thought about her abduction or finding the mystery man... Truth be told it was a good feeling. Perhaps everyone else had been right, and her imagination was playing tricks on her. It was easier to think of a benevolent, if weird, kidnapper, than volatile Ward who could snap at any time and had already hurt her.

Ellie shuddered at the memory as she hung her purse on the coat rack and walked into the bathroom where she stood, indecisive for a few moments. She felt like a long, relaxing bath, but she had promised Libby to check in with them tonight. It would have made more sense to stay in the city and meet them later, but she had wanted to come home and change into something other than the clothes she'd put on this morning. She'd rushed in the hope to spend some time with Jordan, dinner maybe, but she wasn't even here.

Ellie was about to leave again when the doorbell rang.

"Oh. Hey. Jordan isn't here."

"Do you have a moment?" Bethany asked, and Ellie resisted the childish impulse to slam the door in her face. She had to find a more adult way to deal with Jordan's ex, be smart about it. There were times, however, when she made Ellie feel uncertain, especially now when she had basically abandoned her apartment and sought shelter with Jordan. She still needed to cancel her lease. Yes, there was the idea she might find another place of her own, but as it was, Jordan wasn't pushing the issue, and so far, they'd been comfortable together. Ellie wasn't comfortable with Bethany knowing she lived here for the time being. She realized she still hadn't answered the question.

"Actually, I don't. I was going to meet someone."

She couldn't imagine what she and Bethany would have to talk about, and she didn't want to find out.

"I only need a few minutes of your time, then I'll be gone," Bethany promised, walking inside. "Thank you so much. I think this will be of interest for you too. It's about your abduction."

⁂

Bethany didn't need to be here, Jordan thought with rising frustration as she let herself into her house. They had worked together on cases in which the perpetrator was a ruthless psychopath, and then it made sense to involve a profiler. Lately, work seemed to be slow for her ex who found the time to hang around all too often, for no good reason.

She walked into the living room where Bethany sat comfortably. Ellie, judging from the sounds, was in the kitchen—preparing something? Goodness. Probably she'd found a way to escape until Jordan returned.

"What's this supposed to mean?" she asked by way of greeting.

Bethany regarded her with the patient expression that never failed to irritate her.

"Hi, Jordan. I can't blame you for being suspicious, but I can assure you, I'm not here for you."

"Okay, what do you want?"

This moment, Ellie entered the room, carrying two coffee mugs.

"It's ready...You're home."

"Yes, I am. Could somebody explain to me...?"

Casting an uncertain glance at Bethany, Ellie said, "I guess we have some vague proof for my theory after all."

There was no doubt as to what she was talking about, and by now, Jordan was interested—and less irritated with Bethany's presence. Tying up those loose ends would go a long way to ease all of their minds. Jordan sat on the side of the armchair Ellie had taken a seat in. "Okay. Tell me more."

"We're interested in your mystery man," Bethany explained cheerfully. "I talked to a few colleagues, and Josh Ward was no stranger. Apparently, he was involved in some bombings earlier this year, empty buildings, insurance fraud, no one got hurt."

"Yeah, I heard about those. Go on."

"Haynes's boss was one of the suppliers. Haynes wasn't always doing the deliveries, but he must have known that Ward was doing business with him."

"Really?" Jordan made the connection in a split-second. "He called him Watts! That's who he must have meant! That's who the order was for. Okay, but Ward was already dead by the time the deal went down. Who was the one who went to pick up the explosives instead? And where's the connection to the second kidnapper?"

"We don't know yet about the buyer. My point here is, Ward was the hired help to just about every criminal in town, which included Haynes, and a number of others. We have a transcript of a voice chat that has him talking about a job he was doing for some other guy, scaring his girlfriend, locking her up in his apartment for a few days. He mentions that she's an officer."

Bethany hesitated for a few heartbeats, before she added, "Said he might even get himself some action during that time."

The color had drained from Ellie's face, but she sat up straight, her voice even, when she said, "He didn't."

Jordan wordlessly took her hand, regardless of the witness to this display of affection.

"I'm sorry," Bethany said. "I thought you guys would like to know about this. It sounds very much like Ward was paid to execute someone else's plan, and that would make a lot of sense. He never works alone. Ellie has been very observant under the most difficult circumstances. I got to take a look at the notes she wrote right after her abduction. It's impressive. You've got competition coming to your floor."

Ellie smiled, self-conscious with the praise from an unusual source.

"I just wish the bastard had taken off his mask once."

Jordan got to her feet, trying to process what she'd heard.

"We will take this back to Haynes. If he knows something about the other guy Ward worked for, hopefully we can convince him to share."

"Yeah, about that. It's certainly worth a try, but Haynes is ours now, obviously. What I can do is try to stall for a bit, so that you get another shot at him."

"Thank you." Owing Bethany might not be the best idea, but Jordan didn't see an alternative in this case. Besides, it sounded like a genuine peace offering.

"I understand the PD had some trouble backing Ellie's theory," Bethany continued. "I know, the resources..." Of course, this was also a chance for her to point out something that was amiss at the department.

"Well, yeah. It's great that someone has those resources. I need to see the transcripts."

Bethany got up as well. "I'll make sure you get them too. Thanks, Ellie."

"No problem. Jordan, would you like a coffee too? I'll be right back."

Ellie didn't wait for an answer, but disappeared into the kitchen, silence ensuing.

"I better get back to work."

"Sure. Bethany...You didn't have to come here, so...thank you."

Bethany shrugged.

"I mean it. It's not in your job description. It was tough on Ellie, with everyone believing that there was never a second man."

"I can imagine. Look, I know it's quite the awkward situation, but that doesn't mean we can't try to be adults about it. I made mistakes I still feel bad about, and I hope you can forgive me one day. Yeah, like it's all about me and my feelings." She laughed ruefully. "I'm glad we found this. There are things I wouldn't wish on my worst enemy, and of course, Harding is far from that. That sounded better in my head. I should go. You'll have those transcripts as soon as I get to a computer."

"Okay. Thanks." Jordan went to see Bethany out. At the door, she hesitated, a clear indication that a part of the conversation wasn't over yet, making Jordan fear there was another detail in the transcript, or something that Ellie hadn't mentioned yet.

"What?"

"Nothing. Take good care of yourself. I know this can't be easy for you."

"I wasn't the one who got abducted," Jordan said automatically.

Bethany's words echoed what she hadn't said out loud. "This time. Regardless of what you might think, yes, I was angry with you for some time, but I don't wish you harm. You started out in this relationship with some pretty heavy stuff."

"Do you ever turn this off?"

Bethany laughed. "Guilty as charged. I guess what I'm trying to say is…There's no reason why we shouldn't ever talk. If there's something on your mind, you can always call me. I want you to know that."

"Thank you."

Jordan returned to the living room where Ellie sat, poring over some notes. Those were copies of the originals she had given Maria Doss, and that Bethany had obviously seen as well. She looked up, giving Jordan an apologetic smile.

"To be honest, I wasn't sure if I should let her in, but this is good news, right?"

"It is. I guess she already told the lieutenant. Bristol maybe, though I'm not sure," Jordan said, sitting next to her. "Are you okay?"

"Me? Why wouldn't I be? There's finally movement, and someone believes in what I said all along."

"I believed you." Truth be told, those words had stung a little, insinuating Bethany had been the first. Then again, her feelings didn't matter so much when she'd been given a reminder of what Ellie had been through.

"Yes, I know," Ellie said softly. "But you kind of have to. Wait, that's not what I meant. I know you were sincere about it, but coming from Bethany, that's a huge vote of confidence. I'm glad about it, not so much about the confirmation that he's still out there."

"We still have little to go on. Apparently, Josh Ward had a lot of 'friends' who hired him for jobs."

"Yes, but maybe we can narrow it down some with the help of the FBI? It's strange, right, but it makes me feel better to know I didn't make him up. I wasn't that scared. He seemed kind of...benevolent in a strange way. Very different from Ward. I was lucky to have the tab from that beer cab, even luckier the other guy came back that moment and he didn't want in. It tells me he might have some decency after all, and that we could communicate with him."

Jordan thought that was a tad optimistic. After all he had drugged and kidnapped Ellie, which was nowhere near any decency, but she could relate to everything Ellie revealed between the lines. Still, Ellie's approach to deal with this experience seemed so calm and rational. She wasn't freaking out, over-exercising or drinking. It worried Jordan that she might not be dealing at all, suppressing her emotions, and Jordan didn't have a clue about how to help her—that after all her visits to shrinks and nine years of living with one.

"Okay. We'll go from here. I'll go back to the department later and check on those transcripts."

"I'll come with you. Oh, and I almost forgot about this, Darla came by earlier...Did you catch up with her?"

"No, I didn't see her. What did she say?"

Ellie looked uncomfortable all of a sudden. Jordan told herself it was cynical to assume Darla might be in trouble. She'd been doing so well since she'd been released from the hospital.

"She wanted to talk to you only, and...she's pregnant. Is it terrible that I thought it might not be planned?" Ellie sighed. "I thought I was better than that, but obviously I'm as judgmental as anyone else."

"Darla really wanted an out. I wonder what happened. I suppose someone would have told me if there was a problem with the program..."

"For all we know, she found a decent guy and they are planning a family together—or maybe she does have another plan. Sometimes I have to remind myself, when it's not the job, it's totally fine to leave people alone. We don't always know what's best for others, and she didn't seem troubled to me."

Jordan wondered if there was a deeper meaning behind Ellie's words, but for the moment, she was still baffled about the news.

"She must have found out when she was in the hospital, or soon after."

Ellie didn't contest that theory.

Jordan had called in quite a few favors so that Darla could leave her old life behind and get her GED while working. Darla was smart and had been eager to get off the streets. Of course, those plans didn't always work out. Jordan had put a lot of faith in her. She owed her, of course, since it was her case, her perp that almost got Darla killed...They might be even now, but it didn't mean she couldn't have an opinion. She knew firsthand what could happen to children of people who weren't ready to be parents.

Ellie was right. Maybe this was all in her head.

꧁

It was with a lot more confidence that Ellie walked into the station—ironic that it was partly because of Bethany. At least, her case would now move forward. The man behind her abduction was no longer a phantom.

Jordan didn't need to feel insecure about her part in keeping Ellie sane during those past days. It had been a relief to be with her.

As promised, Bethany had forwarded the files, and they sat behind Jordan's desk to study them. It was likely that she still felt guilty about the course of the Darby case. Ellie could imagine that she needed to circumvent some interdepartmental bureaucracy to make those transcripts available to them so quickly.

She told herself it was nothing she hadn't known before, a criminal boasting to a friend of his about future endeavors. Still, when she got to the line Bethany had mentioned before, Ellie felt breathless for a moment, with anger, and helplessness at the blatant misogyny. He was talking about her.

"You need a break?" Jordan asked.

"No, let's go on. We don't want to be here all night."

"Okay. We can pick up something for dinner on the way home."

The biggest part of Ward's conversation seemed unrelated—he was talking to the owner of several buildings in the city that had gone up in flames, a man now in FBI custody.

The man in between was Troy Haynes, Ellie reflected, some-one known to Ward, who had been trying to make a deal earlier that was unrelated to the insurance fraud. The one who got away—was he planning something even bigger than blowing up empty buildings? It was a chilling thought. The deal hadn't gone through this time, but the "scrawny guy" was still an unknown figure.

Like that friend of Ward's who had pretended that Ellie was his girlfriend.

The room looked exactly like the last time she'd seen it. The cot with the cuffs dangling from it, a blanket, on the other side, a small table and lamp. The tiny window, too high and too small to serve as an escape route. She remembered all of it, the feel of the coarse fabric covering her, the cuff biting into her wrist.

She couldn't breathe or move, making a choked gasp in the futile attempt to get some air into her lungs.

"Don't worry, this will only hurt for a little while," he said, pressing the sharp end of the tab into her skin. She saw the blood drip down her shirt, pain registering full force, but the scream didn't come.

Instead, Jordan woke from the nightmare, coming face to face with Ellie's wide-eyed alarmed expression. She remembered trying to scream, and, embarrassed, wondered if she actually had.

"Are you all right?" Ellie asked quietly.

Jordan held up her hand to ward off any questions and attempts at consolation, got up and headed for the bathroom. Her shirt was sticking to her skin, and she threw it into the hamper with more force than necessary, aware that her hands were still shaking. She hated feeling this way, only slowly extracting herself from the grip of the nightmare. A quick shower would keep it at bay, this time. She couldn't afford to dwell on this. It was over, for both of them.

When she returned to the bedroom, Ellie had turned on the light. "Can I get you anything, a tea maybe or..."

"No. Go back to sleep. It's fine."

"Jordan."

She dropped the towel and chose a shirt and panties from the drawer, putting them on before she slipped back under the covers.

"I mean it. Come on, it's nothing big. Let's try to get some sleep."

Jordan had no desire to explain how the images from the claustrophobic room had become mixed up with the memory of Darby's basement. Chances were, Ellie could guess. She looked doubtful but got back into bed and hesitantly scooted closer.

"It's okay," Jordan said.

"You're shaking. You were so far away...For a moment, I was afraid to touch you."

"I'm sorry. I didn't mean to freak you out. I've had nightmares before."

"Do you want to talk about it—this one?"

"No." Jordan wrapped her arms around Ellie tightly and kissed her. "Good night."

⁂

She snuck out of the house early and met with Darla before her shift. In the past, Jordan had often invited her to a sweet coffee and pastry treat, and it seemed Darla still appreciated this sort of food.

"Don't worry," she said, "I'll pay this time. Also, I have to eat for two now, so there's a good excuse."

Jordan had had trouble falling back asleep the night before, and even without the unwelcome reminder of past horrors, her patience was running low.

"Okay. Tell me what happened?"

"Well, it's obvious what happened, isn't it? I mean, you like girls, but you know..."

At this point, Jordan was feeling like indulging in lots a caffeine and empty calories too. This day could only get better—hopefully.

"Yes, I do know the basics, thank you. What I would like to know is what your plan is. You found out about this in the hospital?"

Darla nodded. "I didn't want to share this with anyone right away. I mean...this is kind of a miracle, right? Ryder's people left me for dead, and I would be if it wasn't for those girls who found me. Now, I'm going to have a baby."

It was hard to argue with Darla's logic, still, Jordan wasn't sure if this was a reason to celebrate. There was a lot at stake for Darla.

"Does Sophia know?"

"Sure, I kind of had to let her know. Serena came by one time, and I wanted to tell you...I hoped you'd be happy for me. Happier than Sophia, anyway."

Jordan imagined that the social worker whom she'd contacted for Darla would not be amused. "Well, she knows a lot more about what it's like to raise a child on a budget. You're going to drop out of the program?" That came out a lot sharper than intended. Or maybe it was exactly what she'd intended. She'd wanted Darla to be one of her success stories.

"Of course not," Darla protested. "Hey, this is all going well for me. I'm not going to mess it up if that's what you think."

"Seems to me you already have." Perhaps Ellie had the better attitude about this, trying not to judge until she had all the information. Dealing with her own birthmother who had been too young and completely unfit to start a family, the situation felt personal to Jordan. Especially when for a long time, she'd hoped to be able to help Darla start over.

"Gee, someone got up on the wrong side of the bed today. What's the matter with you? I'm not asking you for money. I got this."

"What about the father?"

Darla rolled her eyes. "We all make mistakes, huh? It doesn't matter anymore. That was in the old life. This is the new me, classes, job, and all. I'm having this baby, and I'm going to get my degree and get a decent job to support us."

"Darla, it's not that easy to raise a child."

"Oh really, and how would you know?"

Jordan told herself she wouldn't be tempted to flee from a conversation with a young woman who'd had fewer lucky breaks in life. She had to make her see what she was getting herself into.

"I was in the system for a while because my birthparents had no idea what the hell they were doing. It wasn't fun."

"Well, I'm sorry about that, but that's not what's going to happen to my little one. I was going to tell you I'm grateful for all that you've done for me, but I didn't realize there were conditions, that it's only okay as long as you approve of what I'm doing with my life. I'm sorry I bothered you. I'll stick to Sophia in the future."

"Darla, wait..."

Darla tossed a bill on the table and got up. "I need to go to class. Bye."

That went well. Jordan shook her head, wishing she had found better words to warn Darla—or kept her mouth shut.

Chapter Twelve

On their way to the squad car, Kate and Ellie passed by a small group of uniformed officers outside the building, most of which were familiar. Ellie had noticed the conversations coming to an abrupt halt when she and Kate walked by. Kate didn't mention it. In fact, she didn't talk much at all even when they were out on the street.

Ellie had her own troubling thoughts, but she still felt bad for breaking her promise.

"I'm sorry. I said I'd be there last night, but when I got home, Dr. Roberts came by to talk about a case...my case actually."

"Doesn't this suck, dating at work, with the exes always around?" Kate sighed. "I guess you heard. It would have been hard to keep a secret, with Jordan practically walking in on us."

"She didn't talk, just...to me," Ellie admitted.

"Yeah, I suspected, and that's okay. I know you're not gossiping about me, but these things get around faster than you can say 'none of your business, guys.' So much for the brotherhood—it's only for sisters when they say so."

"It's not all of them," Ellie assured her. "Those who gossip will find something new soon."

"Sure. I didn't want this to reach Jensen's family because...I don't expect them to understand. I'm not entirely sure I understand it, but sometimes you have to be with someone in a way that's easy and not complicated. I loved Jensen. I still can't wrap my mind around the fact that he's gone, and I don't ever want to feel that way again."

"I understand." That didn't mean she agreed. Ellie didn't know how to be in a relationship without investing all. She'd been disappointed before. She was still convinced that it was worth it overcoming fear and doubts. She wasn't in Kate's shoes though and didn't want to think about how close she'd come once. No wonder Jordan still had nightmares.

With Ward dead, and the mystery man finally on everyone else's agenda as well, Ellie's situation was a completely different one.

"You'll figure it out," she said. "Believe me, they'll stop talking the moment they find something new, and no one should be telling you what to do or how to feel."

"Thank you." Kate gave her a grateful smile. "It's not like I don't have enough to deal with at the moment. I canceled the lease on my apartment because Jensen and I were going to move in together, of course, and now...The landlord was pretty great about it, saying I could stay until I find something new, but I'm sure he expects me to search for a place. Frankly, I haven't. I come home from the shift, I spend some time at the *Code 7*, I sleep and start all over again. I don't want to think. I guess that's how I ended up in a new relationship."

This was an uncomfortable subject for Ellie, as she had unsolved housing issues as well. Doing nothing was a comfortable solution for the time being, but she couldn't continue forever. Deep down she knew it was too early for her and Jordan to take the plunge, that they had to tread carefully if they wanted their relationship to work in the long run, not make early, predictable mistakes.

"You can't always plan these things," she said. "The last few months were rough. Maybe you and I should move in together."

Kate cast her a quick, surprised sideways look. "I thought you were going to stay with Jordan."

"Yes...no. I don't know," Ellie confessed. "It's complicated. I know for sure that I don't want to go back to my apartment, too many crappy memories, and it's too much space and rent for me. I've been putting this off forever. Jordan won't say anything, but it's not easy for her either."

"I guess if I found out that my father was a murderer, I'd need a moment to let that sink in. Would you really want to do that? Get a place together until things are back to something resembling normal?" Kate shook her head. "Not that I have any idea what that state would look like. I know I have to do something."

"Let's try this, then."

"Are you sure? I'd like that, but only if I know you're not going to leave again after a couple of weeks."

"I'll talk to Jordan," Ellie promised, and then dispatch came on, alerting them to a hit and run accident near the city center. She answered the call, glad that the air was clear between her and Kate. She and Jordan would be fine, too—if Ellie could have an adult, work-related conversation with Bethany, then everything was possible.

⁂

Jordan didn't often pay unannounced visits to Jack and Pauline. She could tell Pauline was startled when she opened the door—given the events of the past few weeks, she certainly had reason to be.

"Don't worry, nothing bad happened," Jordan assured her ruefully. Compared to other times, anyway.

"That's a good start. Come on in. I'm glad to see you. Do you have the day off?"

"No, I'll go in later. I've got some overtime left, but Ellie and I want to reschedule the vacation as soon as possible."

"Of course," Pauline said. "You both need it. You've been working hard these past years, and I get the sense that she's the same. You think you could make time for dinner sometime soon? I'm so glad she's okay."

In the kitchen, she poured coffee for both of them. Now Jordan wished she hadn't had breakfast with Darla, as she could have enjoyed Pauline's freshly baked cookies. Even so, sitting with her in the kitchen was calming her nerves, replacing nightmarish memories with good ones.

"Yeah, me too. I keep going back to that night...I wish she'd spent the night at my house instead."

"You couldn't know, and neither did she. I guess it's best to move on. You can't blame yourself."

"I guess." Jordan shrugged, picking up her mug. "I try. We do. There's a lot happening on the sidelines. Kathryn Larson keeps calling me, and I really don't want to forgive and forget. A girl that I helped get off the streets is now pregnant."

Even with Pauline's silence, Jordan could tell right away how she'd gotten this wrong, how she'd let the anger she felt for Kathryn cloud her judgment when it came to Darla.

"I was a real bitch to her, suggesting she couldn't handle it. I think I owe her an apology."

"You were worried. I'm sure she understands."

"I'm not sure I made that clear to her. I don't know...maybe I'm..." She laughed, as the thought struck her as absurd. "Jealous? A few weeks ago, a baby at a crime scene puked on me. No, I'm definitely not jealous of that."

"Would you want a child? You never mentioned it."

"No...maybe, I don't know. My life is not exactly child-friendly, and I'd worry I'd screw it up just as much. Right now, it's impossible to even think of it. Ellie put up with so much, I don't want to scare her away."

"Well, maybe she won't be scared after all. As for Kathryn, you have to figure out what it is you want, what would make you feel better. I agree that you don't owe her anything, but you could have that talk and find out there's nothing to worry about. You're nothing like her as a person, and you'd be a great mother."

Jordan shrugged. "I'm not too sure about that, but it doesn't matter right now. Kathryn is trying, I have to give her that, even it's a bit too late."

"Nothing from Jim."

"No. No surprise here either. He didn't care before he knew about Kathryn's affair, obviously he doesn't now. I gave up on them a long time ago. I wish Kathryn would see that and leave me alone. I have enough on my plate right now."

"Oh, honey, I know."

Jordan hated crying in front of other people regardless, but if it had to happen, she imagined the only woman she felt comfortable calling her mother, qualified.

***

He was starting to believe that every single cop and criminal in the city was beyond incompetent. While that was helpful to Danny at the moment, his frustration was growing. They should welcome him with open arms—the cops, not the criminals, though the encounter had been interesting as well—when he was so much smarter than all of them.

He should be spending his evening chasing after bad guys like Troy Haynes instead of handing out drinks and washing glasses.

His time would come, no matter how much others had tried to prevent it.

Danny couldn't help the unsettling feeling that Josh Ward was mocking him even from the grave—or was it those cops that were mocking him, seeing him as nothing but the guy who provided their drinks night after night? They would learn, all of them.

The big day was approaching fast, and he decided that he didn't need the two idiots who had agreed to meet with him because of his connection with Ward. He didn't get all of the merchandise, and they were going to cheat him on the price as well, but he had enough of the explosives to move on. He could do it all by himself, thanks to the excellent resources on the Internet.

Chapter Thirteen

E llie managed to catch up with a tired looking Jordan at the end of her shift. Given the subject she felt she had to bring up as soon as possible, she suggested going home right away. Home, it was a precarious term. Was tonight the right moment? If she chose to wait, when would be the right time?

"My car or yours?" she asked. Practical things first.

"Mine. I can give you a ride tomorrow."

"I spoke to Kate today," Ellie said. "Some of the guys are giving her a hard time because...you know."

"Yeah, I know." Jordan seemed to ponder this for a moment before she asked, "Did you ever get any of that crap because of us?"

"Not really. It's a different situation. Not that it makes it right," Ellie hurried to say. "I mean, it's not fair. It's bullying. They don't know her."

"I agree, but they'll stop eventually, as soon as they find someone new to pick on."

"True, that's what I said. She's looking for a place to rent right now, which made me think...I have to make a decision about my apartment as well." Ellie took a deep breath. A moment of bravery, and she'd be done with it. "I was thinking of moving in with her. I need to make a decision sooner or later, and I can't exploit your generosity forever. I mean...You know what

I mean. This was meant to be temporary, right? Not us...The living arrangements. So, we have time to figure it all out." She wasn't sure if that made any sense to Jordan, as she had trouble finding sense in her ramblings. Fortunately, Jordan let her off the hook easily.

"That sounds like a good idea," she said.

"You'll be okay with this?" It was almost too easy. Ellie admitted to herself that she might have hoped for an offer, and they would decide together that it was too early for that. She couldn't blame Jordan though. After everything that happened, she couldn't allow herself to make mistakes, with her future, with theirs.

"Sure. I think it's good for the two of you."

Ellie wanted it to be good for Jordan too, so the patience that was so hard to muster would mean something for both of them in the end.

"Okay," she said. "We just came up with the idea, but I guess we'll be looking at apartments soon."

At the red light, Jordan took her hand. "It's okay," she said softly. "If that's what you need right now, that's what we're going to do."

Need, want, not always the same thing. Ellie wanted to hide out at Jordan's as long as she possibly could, but she was aware that it wouldn't do their relationship any good. They were both handling difficult subjects at the moment. Jordan needed space to do so. Ellie needed not to be alone, so under the circumstances, it would be best to go along with the idea.

"We'll try to find something that's not too far from your place, and of course you can still stay over. Okay...how was your day?"

Jordan made a non-committal sound. "First of all, you might have heard Bethany and a colleague are going to join us tomorrow for a meeting. They might have new information on scrawny guy too—you know how they can pull that out of the hat sometimes."

That wasn't the whole story, Ellie understood quickly. Of course, every once in a while, Bethany might be around in a professional capacity, and if she sensed an opportunity otherwise, she'd go for it. They were over that. After those recent confrontations with violent, deluded men, Jordan's ex was the least of their problems.

"Did you have time to see Darla? You never said."

"I did." Jordan sighed. "God, when did I turn into that nasty, judgmental bitch? Sure, it's going to be tough for her, and she could have made better choices, but I was too hard on her."

"You care," Ellie offered. "Talk to her. Apologize. I'm sure she understands. She knows the past months haven't been easy for you either." Jordan's expression told her she was walking a fine line. Nightmares, difficult adjustments, Jordan didn't like to be reminded of how traumatic the recent past had been. Ellie could sympathize. She had worked hard getting over the attack, coming to a point where she'd thought she succeeded after Darby was put behind bars—only to realize the man who'd attacked her had been out there all this time, and his accomplice still was. A kidnapper. Someone possibly planting bombs. Sometimes she wondered why she hadn't become an accountant instead.

"I will. By the way, Pauline asked when we'll be coming for dinner the next time. Would next weekend be okay with you?"

"It's perfect."

Everything would go back to some sort of order. They deserved it. If nothing else, it was that attitude that had brought Ellie here, surviving her captivity, being with the woman she loved. In her opinion, it was worth holding on to. Maybe she didn't have to approach any heavier subjects yet.

135

Ellie was still asleep when Jordan reluctantly disengaged herself from the warm embrace and bed to head for the shower. She wasn't looking forward to her day for many reasons, her apology to Darla the least of it. Talking to Pauline and Ellie had driven the message home. She had overreacted, and she knew it. The upcoming meeting—maybe not pleasant, but they had to move forward with the case. Bethany had been polite and civil when she had come to see Ellie. If she could help them with Haynes, if they got to uncover some information about the other suspect in Ellie's case, they'd go with it.

Kathryn was another subject. She couldn't keep ignoring her and hope she'd just go away. Maybe she had to talk to her, make it clear beyond a doubt that she didn't care for her or Jim in her life. It wasn't a matter of petty payback. It was simply too late to change the habits of a lifetime.

Jordan had dressed and nearly dried her hair when her musings came to a place where she couldn't find clarity so easily. A couple of days ago she'd been worried about feeling crowded. Now that Ellie had come to some conclusions on her own, she should be relieved. Jordan was still waiting for the feeling, and so far, it hadn't come. She was disappointed, not in Ellie, but herself, for not making Ellie feel more welcome, for fearing what happened with Bethany might happen again, simply because Jordan was destined to screw up a relationship no matter what.

Damn, she needed that vacation.

When she came out of the bathroom, coffee was brewing, and Ellie was setting the table. Would it be too much to say she'd miss this?

"Don't worry," Ellie said, as if reading her thoughts. "I'll still make sure that you eat on a regular basis. We'll make this permanent someday, when we're ready." She poured coffee for the both of them and sat down. "We both did this, moving in with someone too quickly, right? We know better now."

Let's hope so.

They didn't continue the subject on the way to the station. Jordan let Ellie drive, lost in her own thoughts.

The pieces coming together were apparently directly related to Ellie's abduction, in a puzzling way. There had been no ransom or attempt at blackmailing. Fortunately, the kidnapper didn't seem to have the same sick obsession with Ellie as Darby had with her—but there were still the text messages. A diversion? Why? At this point, she hoped Bethany and her colleagues would come up with one of their magic tricks, no matter who ended up collecting the laurels. She wanted that kidnapper off the streets, so they could move on with their lives.

In different homes, as Jordan had made it clear without even trying.

At the station, she and Ellie went separate ways. A few minutes later, Jordan caught up with Sergeant Bristol in the hallway, and they walked into the already slightly crowded conference room, the lieutenant, Bethany and a colleague, a couple of uniforms. Maria and Derek sat on opposite ends of the table. Ellie came rushing in just before Bristol almost closed the door in her face. She cast Jordan a quick smile before she sat with Casey.

"I think everyone's here now," Bethany said. "Most of you already know what this is about. Troy Haynes is in federal custody now, as his little local deal is likely to have wider implications."

Jordan shared a look with Derek, and he shrugged. This wasn't common knowledge then.

"Thanks to Haynes, we now know that the man we're looking for was related to your guy Ward."

Ellie shivered.

"Now we don't have to worry about Ward anymore, but he acted as a middleman to many deals, drugs, guns and, lately, explosives. Troy tells us that the C4 you found at the scene wasn't all. Obviously, he didn't get paid for it, but the guy Ward sent him got away with some of the merchandise anyway, and it looks like he has some plans with it. It's enough to bring down a building or two. Let's find him first."

"So, Josh made this deal while he worked with Ellie's kidnapper, and he arranged for them to come here. What was his plan? More insurance fraud?" Jordan asked.

"That's where the timeline doesn't seem to add up," Bethany said. "There wasn't enough time. Ward was a contact of Haynes's boss, but he made the order for someone else. The man who wanted the C4 probably hasn't given up on his plans, so we need to be extra vigilant, especially during the holiday celebrations."

Her words let an uncomfortable silence settle over the group, as the possible worst-case scenario registered with each of them.

"Ward ordered the C4 for someone, but when he got himself killed, that person showed up to finalize the deal," Jordan finally said. "No hint at all as to who he could be? No chatter?"

Bethany shook her head. "We have this one interesting cross-reference, and that's the guy who hired Ward to kidnap Officer Harding. Ward was known for boasting about his 'accomplishments' as we saw him do in the transcripts...If he was involved in something big, he'd be likely to tell—and this other guy was someone he was working with at the same time. So, we're very interested in finding the second man in the abduction."

Ellie sounded frustrated when she spoke. "I've been wracking my brain ever since the day I got out. His voice sounded somewhat familiar, but I still can't put my finger on it. The apartment—it was pretty modest, not a lot of furniture, as if he did rent it for a temporary purpose only. I've been going over every place I went in the past weeks since the texts started. I didn't meet anyone new, I didn't notice anything different. I wish I could help more."

"You already did." Bethany's voice was unusually soft, reminding Jordan why she hadn't always resented her. She appreciated her being professional, genuinely sympathetic when dealing with Ellie. There was hope for the future after all.

"Most importantly, I want all of you to be careful with what information you share outside the meeting. What we do know is that the kidnapper must have been watching Harding for some time, got close to her. Officially, we're looking for Haynes' contact now, the 'scrawny guy,' that is all. No mention of the C4 that got lost. I'll be working closely with Officer Harding."

You will?

Jordan wasn't sure if she appreciated this turn of events. Ellie looked uncertain too.

"I'll do whatever I can to help, but like I said, there's nothing much. I went to the same places, hung out with the same people..."

"Exactly. If no one noticed anything or anyone new, there has to be a reason."

"Wait a minute," Derek interjected. "Dr. Roberts, you're not saying that Harding was abducted by a cop?"

"At this point, this would be speculation," Bethany said coolly. "This guy chose her for a reason, and I think her profession is a likely one. He's close to cops, has a beef with them for whatever reason—he could be one. This is the reason why I want you to keep quiet about what we're talking about here. I'll be in direct contact with your supervisors. You'll be in the loop—until we find Haynes' buyer, we need to be careful. That would be all for now. Do you have any other questions?"

Of course, when Bethany was involved, nothing could ever be easy, though this time it wasn't her fault.

"I have a few phone calls to make," Jordan said. "I'd like to talk to Mercer again and see if he can tell us anything else about Ward. Maybe some of those contacts go way back, from the time Ward had the fallout with his parents." She'd be the first to know about how early experiences would come back to haunt a person, the people you crossed paths with, the damage they could do even much later on. Ward, however, had made his own choices, and one of them was the alliance with Ellie's stalker. Mercer who had successfully painted himself as the only innocent party, might have more answers if she managed to jog his memory.

Meanwhile, Bethany was planning to do the same with Ellie.

"Sure, you do that," Bethany said. Jordan caught the lieutenant frown behind her back, wondering if the men in the room were actually still cautious on her behalf, or Ellie's, or if they simply had trouble seeing a woman taking charge like this. Many men had, no matter how well-meaning and informed.

"Okay. See you later."

There was no reason for her to stay behind, though she felt uncomfortable wondering how Bethany would want to work with Ellie. She was a seasoned psychiatrist, but she was also goal oriented, and Jordan knew Ellie was vulnerable still even though she chose to act as if her abduction had been no big deal. She hoped Bethany would carefully weigh the risks against the benefits. Then she had no more excuse. Darla didn't answer her cell phone, Jordan hoped she was in class right now. She called Sophia, the social worker, next, catching her in her office.

"Jordan, hi, what can I do for you?"

"I saw Darla earlier."

There was a brief moment of silence on the other end of the line. Jordan hoped that this would not spell trouble for Darla.

"Yes, she told me you two talked. Listen, Jordan—I know you worry, but she's handling the situation pretty well." The awkward pause made her wonder how much Darla had told about their argument.

"When will she be coming in? There's something I need to tell her."

"Tomorrow afternoon," Sophia said. "I know this is a surprise, but I can assure you, Darla has done exceptionally well."

"You think she's capable of raising a child?"

There was another pause, before Sophia said, "I know where you're coming from, but unless this is relevant to any police business, I'd like to stop it here. If she doesn't want to go into details with you, I shouldn't. She's doing everything right."

It certainly wasn't meant to sound like a reproach, though to Jordan, it did. For the way she'd handled the news, and to a more irrational part of hers, for the way she was currently handling her life.

Thank God Ellie was patient.

The same couldn't be said of Derek who was making signs that she interpreted as "time to leave." Just as well. She'd see Darla tomorrow and postpone that conversation with Kathryn.

❧

Ellie regarded Bethany dubiously. Having a polite conversation with Jordan's ex was one thing. They all wanted the same thing—catch "scrawny guy"—but this latest suggestion caught her off guard.

"I'm not sure about that," she said.

"Why not give it a try? Let's face it, everyone's watching you right now, wondering if you're okay to do the job."

"I am more than—"

"Relax. I don't doubt that." It wasn't until that moment Ellie realized she'd jumped to her feet.

"You know how it is," Bethany continued. "I'm sure you'll be fine, but you can't deny there's some scrutiny, and it's true, you came back to work soon. With what I'm suggesting, you can help the case, and that will be good for your career. Everyone will move on eventually."

"You want to hypnotize me?" Ellie asked, still skeptical.

"It's not like in the movies. You say you didn't notice anything, anyone new approaching you, but don't forget you were already under a lot of stress. A colleague of yours died, you were worried about Jordan..."

It might be a bait...or not. Either way, Ellie didn't want to go there.

"So what?"

"Maybe I could help you remember. You know that you can't be hypnotized against your will, right? I can assure you, even if I could do that, I'm not interested in details of your relationship with my ex-girlfriend. Promise."

"I wasn't thinking that," Ellie mumbled.

"Good. I went over your notes again. We can do this. We can go across the street to my hotel—it's quieter than the police station, and you'll be less distracted."

"What if I never met him, and I don't have any helpful memories?"

"You might remember more details about him, your captivity. I swear I'm not going to make you waste your time, or the Bureau's. I have helped many witnesses like that."

She called her a witness, not a victim. Ellie had to give her that, even though she still thought of going to a hotel room with Bethany as beyond strange.

"Okay. Let's do this." The moment she said it, she could feel her heart beating faster. She had to trust in Bethany's experience, that this wouldn't be anything out of a Hitchcock movie. Bethany wasn't interested in her childhood—nothing bad to find there—or the time she'd grieved for her parents. Together, they would focus on the time she'd spent locked up and cuffed to the wall in a dark room.

What could go wrong?

Ellie wasn't afraid, or at least that's what she told herself. She had no reason to be. She had made it out of that small stuffy room with little more than a few scratches on her, most of which she got when falling down those damn stairs. She had given an extensive statement, backed by her even more extensive notes, and she was back at work. Not long from now, she and Jordan would go on their much-deserved vacation, for real this time.

She knew what lingered in the darkness, the *what if?* Terrible things could have happened, if she didn't have that small substitute for a weapon, or the other man hadn't returned when he did.

What if? was a terrible way to live your life. Jordan didn't do it, Ellie wouldn't either. There was nothing left to worry about. Bethany didn't care about intimate details, or maybe she did, but she wouldn't let that color her approach. Whatever it took to solve the case—this was where they understood each other.

Something nagged at the back of her mind though as they were standing in the suite of a rather comfortable size.

"You're not staying at the apartment?" This was probably none of her business and an awkward attempt at making small talk, delay the inevitable.

Bethany remained unfazed by her question.

"I don't know if Jordan told you this, but I'm going to move out," she said. "I have no reason anymore for a permanent address around here, if you must know."

"Oh. I see."

"Now that we got this covered, I'd like you to sit down, get comfortable. We'll go over the past few weeks—the time we know Ward rented the apartment where you were held—and slowly get to the main event. I want you to know we can stop this at any time if it gets too much."

"We're not trying to solve the case at any cost?" Ellie inquired. In hindsight, a few seconds later, she wasn't quite sure where these words had come from. It seemed that whenever she felt like getting somewhere with Bethany, she remembered her conduct in Darby's case.

Bethany sat in a chair across from her.

"No, we're not," she said firmly. "I know what you're talking about, but believe me, I learned my lesson. I had some stern conversations with the lieutenant, Bristol, my own supervisor. In the end, I was cleared. I swear I didn't know he was going after Jordan so soon, and this will haunt me for the rest of my life. Is there anything else you want to know before we start?"

"No. I'm fine."

"Okay then, let's get started. I'd like to tape this if it's okay with you?"

"Of course. Whatever I can do to help."

Ellie knew she would regret this at some point, soon, but she also knew how much depended on her. Bethany was right to assume the man who had kidnapped her didn't come out of nowhere. She wished she'd seen him coming earlier when there had still been a chance to turn it all around.

This was everyone's attempt at damage control before something even worse happened.

Chapter Fourteen

"Oh God, this is going to get worse, right?" Michael Mercer shook his head after the detectives laid out the situation to him. "I tried my best to keep my distance from Josh. After he realized that there was no turning back with his parents, he used every opportunity to make money, drugs, guns, girls, whatever he could get involved in. Tucker, he got himself out, I hear, but for Josh, that was never an option. He wanted to make it big. I guess that's why he's dead now." He hunched his shoulders. "That was a long time ago though."

"It wasn't a long time ago when Tucker asked you for the car," Jordan reminded him.

"Yeah, but even he didn't know what Josh was going to use it for, right? He had gone off the deep end, getting involved with people who blow things up? I don't know anything about it, and frankly, I never wanted to. I didn't ask questions."

"Yet you gave him the car. He didn't give you any indication what he needed it for. Somehow, I find that hard to believe."

"Well, I didn't think he would pull his usual bullshit with his new friend, the cop, around. Guess I was wrong."

Jordan cast a quick look at Derek, realizing this was as much of a surprise for him.

"A cop? Why didn't you tell us the first time? Or when our colleagues followed up with you?"

He shrugged. "I forgot. It just came to me, the other guy was wearing a sweatshirt with the PD's logo. Jesus, how was I supposed to know what Josh was up to? I have a life. I can't think of every little detail. You can buy this kind of gear. Or maybe the guy stole the shirt from someone. Come to think of it, now that makes sense."

Or it actually belonged to someone working with them every day, watching Ellie up close. The thought made Jordan sick to her stomach.

"Did you ever hear the name Troy Haynes mentioned?"

"I don't think so, no."

"Okay then. We'll be in touch, Mr. Mercer."

"Yeah, that's what I was afraid of. I got your card already."

As they walked to the car, Derek said, "Seems like Dr. Roberts could be right. Someone hanging out with cops...or a cop."

"I'd prefer the former. What a mess," Jordan summed up the situation. "We have to go over Ward's past, every arrest record, see who worked those cases."

"You really think that one of us was involved in Ellie's abduction? That's still a big stretch."

"I agree, but I hate to say Bethany's instincts are usually right on the money."

"Like they were with Darby."

"Well, okay, not something I'd like to think about now. Let's go do some research now and find Bethany and her colleague after—and let's see what Maria is at." She noticed the minute hesitation on Derek's part and sighed. "All right. I'll see what she's at. At some point you'll have to talk to each other again."

"It's complicated."

Jordan had no doubt. If there was anything she could relate to, it was complicated. Maybe later, over a beer at the *Code 7*, she'd ask him his opinion on Kate and Ellie moving in together.

For now, they'd both feel better if they could rule out any colleague's involvement in Ellie's abduction.

An image of Jonathan Darby flashed in her mind. There was something strangely comforting about being able to distinguish without a doubt good and evil. It wasn't always that easy.

﹏

"Relax. You're safe here. Nothing can happen to you. Tell me what you see."

Ellie took what they were doing seriously. She knew that there was no way in hell Bethany would even be spending time with her if this wasn't important, and yet she couldn't help thinking of this situation as absurd. She also had this unpleasant feeling in the pit of her stomach, like something was going to happen. She wasn't too far off, as Bethany had asked her to go to a time before the kidnapping. Ellie had been on high alert for a while, after the attack, what Darby had done to Jordan, the shooting that left Kate's fiancé dead. No wonder she'd been on edge for so long, always waiting for the next, worst thing to happen.

"If someone has been watching you, it's likely that they've done so for a while." Bethany's voice was soft, alluring. "Tell me about the time after Officer Baker was killed. You all pulled together." Against all odds, Ellie didn't find it hard to follow that voice, regardless of the chilling memories Bethany was invoking. It was safe to look at them from a distance.

"It's a depressing atmosphere," she said. "Everyone's still shocked. We go to the *Code 7* after work, but hardly to wind down. It's tough to be alone and think that this could have been any of us. And we all miss him."

"I understand. Try to think of one night at the *Code 7*. Take a look around. See who's there, who you're talking to."

"Kate. Libby and...Jordan, of course. Wes. Roth, the owner, gives out some drinks on the house. He still does that from time to time. You know he used to be a cop. What do you think this is going to achieve?" Ellie asked, feeling irrationally angry all of a sudden. "He's not there, and if he is, I have no idea who he is."

"We don't know that," Bethany said softly. "Now let's go to the night before you were supposed to go on vacation. At this point, he has everything in place, and he knows where you're going, your schedule. You went to the *Code 7* that night?"

"He must have known." The thought sprang to mind, and it made her stomach clench. "The two of them, Ward and the other guy, I don't know how they are connected, but he must have known about the attack. Maybe he was even watching."

"But you didn't walk home the night before you were taken?"

"No. Jordan drove me, and she was going to pick me up a few hours later to go to the airport. I still had some things to pack—and I thought I could get a few hours of sleep." That night, Ellie had felt light and happy in expectation of the days to come, sun, beach, sex between the cool sheets of a pricey hotel room.

It never happened.

"Take your time," Bethany instructed. "You're home, packing, getting ready to get a few hours of sleep. What happened next?"

"I don't know!"

"There's a part of you that knows. Every little detail can help."

"I don't know anything. He drugged me while I was asleep."

"You were never conscious, not even for a moment?"

The flash, a split-second, came unexpected. Ellie's right hand went to the fingers of the left, where she had cut herself...when? The world was tilting upside down, her fingers hurt, and she was feeling sick.

148

"Breathe. He's not here now. It's just you and me. Did you see his face?"

"He was wearing a mask the whole time. He didn't want me to see his face—or hear his voice. He tried not to speak to me at all, but he couldn't go through with it. Then he tried to alter his voice but didn't stick to it either."

"Do you remember his voice? Did you hear it, at the *Code 7*, at the station, at any time before you woke up in the apartment?"

"I don't know!"

"I know you're frustrated. I understand. Be patient. It will come to you."

"It hasn't come to me in all this time, what makes you think it will change?" Ellie opened her eyes and jumped to her feet, surprised at the wave of vertigo. "This was a big waste of time. There's nothing more."

"Allow me to disagree—but first sit down for a moment." Bethany opened the curtains before she picked up a glass of water from a side table. "Here, take a few minutes before we go back to the department. Jordan texted me. It seems that she and Henderson have found something too."

"What?" Ellie accepted the water and sat, but she had no idea why Bethany was this excited. She'd been aware the whole time. There was nothing new. "I didn't remember anything else."

"The sweatshirt? That wasn't in your notes or your earlier statement. It's certainly possible to come by, but much easier for real cops."

"Wait, what are you talking about?"

"You said he was wearing a shirt with the PD's logo at one time, Ellie, do you understand what that could mean? This is why I didn't want anyone outside of the meeting to know about the avenues we were pursuing. It's significant."

"I said that?"

"Don't worry about it." Bethany laid a hand on her shoulder and let it rest there for a moment. Ellie was too baffled to even have a reaction to the gesture. "It's normal. People are responsive to these techniques in varying degrees. We will listen to the recording later. Other little details might come back to you over time. It's not sorcery, I promise, just a way to sort it all out."

Ellie took another sip of the water before she got up. "Thanks, I guess. We have a lot of work to do now."

"No kidding. The sweatshirt wasn't found at the apartment. Its owner made sure that only Ward's name was on the lease, and with Haynes' people. He's hiding somewhere in plain sight. Let's go see what the detectives have and share the results of our afternoon."

"Yeah." Ellie wondered what Jordan would be thinking of those results, and how they had been obtained. She wasn't sure she wanted to know.

"I was scared," she said. Where had that come from?

"Of course. Only a fool wouldn't have been." For what it was worth, Bethany understood. One day, Ellie would like to hear about the first cases she and Jordan worked on together, all those years ago.

"Jordan, a word?"

Jordan wasn't sure what to make of the fact that Bethany and Ellie had come in together, both looking serious. She nodded and got up to follow them into the break room.

"Now what? We're the most secretive of an already secretive group?"

"This is no joke," Bethany chastised her. "Harding came up with something important this afternoon. She remembered the kidnapper was wearing a sweatshirt with the PD's logo."

"Yes, we found out about this, plus Ward was arrested twice only this year by members of this precinct, on drug charges and assault. His record goes way back, even Roth arrested him before."

"That's the owner of the *Code 7*, isn't he?" Bethany asked.

"Yes, but we've been focusing on recent events, back to the time Ellie was attacked the first time. We already talked to Detective Waters. The other arrest was made by Officer Wes Martin."

"He was in my class," Ellie said. "Come on, I would have recognized his voice! He volunteers in soup kitchens and is helping his sister through college. It's not that hard to get one of those sweatshirts."

"Yes, we're aware. Still, there are some irregularities we are currently looking into. Don't worry. We're keeping a low profile."

"Yeah, you better." Bethany miraculously agreed with her, though Jordan hadn't missed the stormy look on Ellie's face.

"You're going to investigate one of my friends?"

"We're going to ask some questions. I think it will be best if you do your job, see if you notice anything unusual. If the guy kept close all this time, chances are he still does, trying to stay low key. We're not accusing anyone."

Yet.

A sweatshirt was definitely not enough to get the young officer into trouble, but some details she and Derek had discovered this afternoon, might.

"All right. Do you need me for anything else?" Ellie asked.

"Actually yes. We are looking at Haynes' people who have done business in town and crossed paths with Ward in the past few years. Doss will give you some details."

Jordan could have done that, but she had to head back to where Derek was having a casual conversation with Officer

Martin, and besides, she wanted to know what Bethany had done with Ellie all afternoon. She told herself this wasn't at all informed by any feelings of unease, or, God forbid, jealousy.

When Ellie had closed the door behind her, she asked, "What was this all about?"

Bethany shrugged. "Work. What do you think? It's not unusual that victims of a crime remember details later. Memory doesn't always work in a linear way, and that detail obviously means something. This guy, wearing a police sweatshirt...it doesn't mean that he *is* a cop, but oddly, for a criminal, he seems to like being associated with the police."

"Or mock us."

"Yes, that's a possibility," Bethany agreed. "In any case, it's no coincidence. Other than that, if you want to ask, do it already so we can all go back to work."

"Ask you what?"

"We didn't talk about anything personal. Frankly, there's no time. I want this guy off the streets before he blows up anything else, and if Ellie's kidnapper can help us with that, two birds with one stone."

"Can't you turn off the shrink for a moment? I didn't expect you to discuss anything personal."

Bethany wasn't at all offended. "She's coping in a very different way, so I hope you're prepared. When you don't want to deal with something, you shut down, close yourself off from everyone. Clearly, that's not her thing. She seems okay, but there's a lot going on under the surface."

"Here we go with the personal...You're worried about me?"

"No. I'm worried about her."

Secretly, Jordan felt the same. Ellie's return to work and life after her abduction had been swift and smooth, maybe a bit too much—and she felt guilty because she knew Ellie was still trying to spare her. By not talking about details. Maybe, by moving out at the first opportunity.

"She'll be fine. Not everyone follows your textbooks."

Bethany laughed. "Now I'm insulted. My job isn't just about textbooks, you know? Anyway, we both have someplace to be now. Good luck, Jordan."

"Thanks."

She could use it, and lots of it.

⁘

Jordan quietly entered the interview room where Derek was sitting with Officer Wes Martin.

"Whatever I can do to help. You want to know about Ward? I remember those guys he hung out with, too," he said, seeming eager. "Mercer, Branson, they both seemed to make an honest effort."

Jordan winced, remembering Branson had tried to hit her over the head with a pipe, trying to escape. So much for an honest attempt. Still, his record looked infinitely better than Josh Ward's.

"Ellie—Officer Harding—arrested Branson once, but I think most of us brought in Ward at one time. I heard that in the beginning, his parents tried to bail him out, but eventually they disowned him. He was heading for disaster. Was there anything wrong with the arrests? Is that why I'm here?"

"No, you didn't do anything wrong," Derek assured him. "Those old cases might be related to a current one, and it's important we go over every detail."

"Is that why the FBI is still in the house? Something big?"

"We went over your reports. Is there anything you remember about Ward...maybe wanting to get back at the police, or did he make any personal threats?" Jordan asked.

"Ward, no. I remember Branson lost it in court back then and yelled at Ellie. Ward never seemed to be the one to instigate. He was always someone's hired help, and that's how he got himself out time after time, turning on others."

If only he was alive to tell the story now, Jordan thought. Who was the mysterious man who had put Ward's name on the lease of the apartment, and what was he up to now? Certainly, the man on the loose with C4 was more worrisome, but Ellie's kidnapper might lead them to him.

"Did you talk about these cases to anyone outside of work?"

Martin looked uneasy as if he was adding up the evidence that this was indeed more than a friendly conversation among colleagues. "Some guys at the bar," he said nervously. "They're all cops."

"That's all right. Do you think someone could have over-heard you, someone who's not a cop?"

"Come on, you talk cases there after a shift, don't you?" Just like that, uneasy became defensive. "Besides, the owner used to be a cop, right?"

"So, you think somebody might have heard something they would have used—against you, or to plan the abduction of Officer Harding?"

Officer Martin shook his head. "I really don't like where this is going. I did nothing wrong. I thought you had a few questions over an arrest record, but this looks like I should get my union rep and a lawyer involved. Does Sergeant Bristol know?"

"I do, Officer."

All eyes went to Bristol standing in the door. "Josh Ward attacked Officer Harding twice. He was arrested and let go only a week before the first time, in her neighborhood. That was your arrest. If you have any other information, now would be the moment to come forward."

"I am not answering any more questions at this point," Martin shot back.

❧

Jordan was late hurrying across the street and into the building that housed Sophia's office. To her relief, she found Darla still in the waiting area, leafing through some information for mothers-to-be. She looked up when Jordan walked in.

"Sophia said you wanted to talk to me," she said, her expression guarded.

"Yeah. Let me buy you a coffee?"

Darla shrugged. "You don't need to buy me food anymore. Believe it or not, I've got a pretty good handle on things, even though you probably can't imagine that."

"Come on. I was out of line. I'm sorry."

"Are you? Sorry, I mean?"

"What do you want me to say? I hope you didn't lose your love for everything sweet, so I have a chance here to make it right. It's not like I can tell you how to live your life."

"I won't be depending on your tax dollars, if that's what you think."

"I don't know what I was thinking," Jordan confessed. "And by the way, you helped me a lot. It's about time you catch a break. I was caught off guard."

"I guess so. I think I even understand, with what you told me. It's not like I didn't have a moment of panic myself, but I have people who support me now. I am not going to screw this up. All right, I won't say no to something sweet, but you probably knew that already. How are you doing after everything?" Darla asked as they left the building and headed towards the café across the street.

"That's a good question. I guess my earlier reaction gave you an answer to that. Parenting is still a touchy subject."

"Yeah, I can imagine. Doesn't mean you wouldn't be doing okay. By the way, you know I met your girlfriend. She's cute. Who is going to have the baby?"

"Whoa, slow down, no one. Your brain is on a one-way street at the moment."

It was true, the revelations about her birthparents had given her some thought, and the sobering reminder that certain windows weren't eternal, but this wasn't the time. She wasn't ready. Ellie was...healing, and according to Bethany, this process had only just started. Unfortunately, Bethany was mostly right when it came to these subjects. Jordan hadn't dealt with her birthmother's attempts at making peace yet, and Ellie was going to move out...

No, she was in no place to judge Darla who, after a long uphill battle, was trying to take control of her life.

"Speaking of which. Chocolate cake would be amazing."

On that, Jordan could agree.

Relieved she'd been able to smooth things over with her former CI, she arrived back at the station to find Ellie was still out, working overtime alongside of Casey. Doss was nowhere to be found, and Officer Martin had sought legal representation. She caught Derek heading out.

"I guess we'll continue here tomorrow," he said. "It looks like Martin does have some secrets, whatever they are."

"Yeah, about that. I talked to Roth a while ago, but I'd like to go see him again. Maybe something comes to mind about Wes, or the people he talked to. Roth is a good observer. He might be able to help us if we ask the right questions, and he once arrested Ward, too. We could even stay for a drink afterwards."

Bethany's warnings rang in her mind. If things were going to get more difficult, she might as well clear the air with everyone she'd gone off on lately, work out her own issues, so she could be there for Ellie if she needed her.

"Sounds like a plan," Derek agreed.

"All right—and I know who you date is none of my business, or anyone else's. I heard some folks are giving McCarthy a hard time. That's not right."

"Who?" he asked, his tone making Jordan wonder if she should have kept that detail to herself.

"I don't know names, I swear. They're just immature. It'll blow over."

"It better. She doesn't deserve that kind of crap."

Jordan silently agreed. She was relieved though that everyone around her seemed to be in a forgiving mood today.

Chapter Fifteen

C arl Roth took it in stride that the police had even more questions for him. He gave Jordan and Derek an apologetic shrug. "I'm sorry I can't help you much. I remember Ward, a nasty little weasel. There was nothing he wouldn't do for money. He'd practically beg people to let him in on a job. I'm not surprised that he got himself killed, but I actually am surprised about the way it happened. I assume he made many enemies over the years. As for your other question—of course I don't know everyone who comes through here, but the majority of them are from the precinct. You know. You could ask Danny though...I haven't been here a lot in the past months, so he might have picked up something. You really think it's someone who's been coming here?"

"Both attacks happened shortly after Ellie and I came here," Jordan said. "It could be a coincidence, but..."

"You don't think so," he finished. "Danny!" he called towards a door in the back. "Can you come here for a second?"

Roth's son was in his early thirties. Everyone had seen him around—he was doing the books and sometimes helping behind the counter. If anything was out of the ordinary, chances were he knew about it.

Jordan tried to remember if he'd been there the night she'd dropped Ellie off at her apartment to do some last minute packing and get a few hours of sleep. She remembered asking Ellie to stay over. Ellie had laughed and claimed she wouldn't get any sleep that way.

"Danny, the detectives are here about Officer Harding's case. They think someone might have been stalking her. Did you notice anything here at the bar, someone watching her maybe?"

"Here, in a room full of cops? I think everyone else would have noticed before me." He gave a nervous sounding laugh.

"Just try," Jordan advised, already put off by his attitude. It had been a long day, with Bethany around and working with Ellie on her memories. In addition to that Jordan had to apologize to pretty much everyone she was close to—not to mention a multitude of other unsolved issues.

"Well, I don't know what to say. I certainly didn't hear anyone say they wanted to kidnap Officer Harding. I thought that first time was the serial killer, are you sure he doesn't have anything to do with this?"

"Believe me, the thought occurred to us," Derek said. Jordan saw Roth wince, but if it was at his son's words, or Derek's reaction, she wasn't sure.

"Well, there was this one guy, he came in every once in a while. I don't know his name, or where he is now...but he did watch the girls. Never spoke to anyone though."

Roth seemed perplexed. "You never mentioned anything about this."

"I didn't think it was important. Some guys are shy...I imagined he went some other place, or maybe he didn't like cops. No offense, guys."

"This might be important," Jordan told him. "Can you describe the guy?"

"I don't know, my age, tall, blond...that's all I remember. I'm sorry. Wait, he had a tattoo...a pair of dice, I think, on his forearm."

"We'll definitely look into that. Anything else?"

"Not that I can think of."

"Okay. Thank you for your time."

"If you need to make a positive ID or anything, you know where to find me." Again the nervous laugh.

This day was long from being over.

"Danny," Roth asked, "before Officer Harding went missing, did you see Josh Ward in here, or close to the building?"

Something about this question, and Roth's tone, struck Jordan as curious. Sure, Roth's son probably had heard about Ward on the news or in the papers, but how would he have identified him before? The only explanation was that he already knew him.

"He wouldn't set foot into the bar," Danny said. "Cops, you know."

"That didn't stop him that one time."

"Dad, stop. They're not interested in that."

"Oh, I am," Jordan said. "Ward was here? When? And why didn't anyone tell us about it?"

Roth sighed. "He was back out of prison again, and Danny was going through a tough time. I didn't want him to get involved with Ward, so I told him to get the hell out and stay away from my son. I never saw him again. It's highly unlikely that there's any connection to your case."

Let me be the judge of that, Jordan thought.

"What did Ward want from you?"

"We never really found out," Roth answered for his son. "I knew for certain that he was bad news, so I sent him packing."

"Is that all?" Daniel Roth asked, clearly uncomfortable. "I need to go back to work."

"For now," Jordan said. "We'll be in touch."

Ward, always in search for a job—or an accomplice?

They were getting closer. He had to move, and fast. As Danny returned to labor over the books he didn't care for to begin with, he felt calm. He could do this, in a matter of days, and finally get to a point where he no longer had to pretend. Danny had the feeling he would be up all night working on his final plan.

It amused him that they all wondered what was so special about Harding, when she'd simply been in the room when he came up with the idea. It could have been any of them. The one who had been engaged to the fallen officer. The older one who was Harding's training officer. Everything about Harding had seemed so convenient, until, of course, Ward decided to be an asshole, and the second time she escaped barefoot and in a nightgown. He probably should have gone for something bigger right away, not waste so much time, but the moment was coming.

After finishing up at the bar, he locked the door and, in the parking lot, sat in his car for a moment, smiling to himself.

He could still be the hero.

After finding some cross references, Ellie and Casey spent the bigger part of the late afternoon knocking on door and talking to residents of the neighborhood where Troy Haynes' and Ward's territory had overlapped. She still couldn't believe Wes had anything to with her abduction. He had asked to switch shifts often, was in the neighborhood whenever possible.

It gave her pause. She still didn't want to believe that someone she'd met at the academy could have been a part of this. How could everyone believe this so easily? Then again, some people she'd thought were friends were calling Kate names behind her back.

"One more address on the list," Casey announced. "It's odd that everyone seemed to know Ward one way or another, but no one believes he could be a mastermind behind any crime. Scrawny man is a ghost just as much as that second guy."

"Believe me, he was very real to me. I'm sorry." Ellie sighed. "I'm tired. We've been at this for hours, and nothing of importance. Maybe Wes's arrests really have nothing to do with any of this. Ward is dead. It's a, pardon the pun, dead-end street."

"Yeah, and mine wasn't a good pun either. Sorry about that. You're doing okay?"

"I guess."

Ellie didn't share that the experience with Bethany had shaken her, the moment she'd slipped away and produced a detail that hadn't entered her consciousness before. It wasn't much in terms of progress for the case, since Jordan and Henderson had found it from a different angle, but it made her wonder what else might linger there.

"I'll be better after we're done here," she said. "Let's see what Jay has to tell us and then head back."

"Yeah, let's do that."

Ellie wasn't especially optimistic, but at least, this would be their last stop. She could probably catch up with Jordan and Kate at the *Code 7* later. She didn't want to go to Jordan's yet or pack up things in her own apartment. A bit of background noise would be helpful.

There was something about the hotel room that had freaked her out, going back to some of the most difficult moments of her life under Bethany's guidance.

Jay Easton, who had been interviewed regarding incidents with both Haynes and Ward, stood on his doorstep, smoking a cigarette. He shook his head when he saw them coming towards him. "Man, this is not a good sign. What do you want?"

"Just talk, Jay, don't worry. Before March 13th, did you see this guy around here?"

Jay took a look at the picture she held up to him. "Ward, that's the guy who was shot in the convenience store? He hung around, looking for jobs. Not that I would know how to help him with that, but yeah, I've seen him around."

"So, what did you tell him?"

"Nothing. We hardly spoke, but there was talk about someone hiring him eventually. For what, I don't know. As I said, we were not in touch, but he always ended up getting some job, because he was cheap."

"Can you tell us where that talk came from?"

"Just folks. I'd tell you if I knew more! I can ask around a bit. I'll let you know as soon as I find something out. If you excuse me now? It's bedtime for my kids."

"Jay," Ellie called after him. "Call us anytime, okay? This is important."

"I figured. Goodnight, Officers."

"Yeah, goodnight," Casey said once he was out of earshot. "This is unbelievable. Why do they all have such selective memory?"

Ellie didn't have an answer for her. She shook herself to get rid of the uncomfortable feeling, something vague and indefinable. She had given out her cell phone number sometimes, not often, but to a few women and children mostly, advising them that 911 was the better alternative if they needed help quickly. Had her number made it into the hands of the stalker that way? Someone's husband, father?

When they entered the *Code 7* twenty minutes later, Kate was waving to her from where she sat at the corner table with Derek.

Jordan was nowhere to be seen, so she headed for her friend's table with her drink.

"Hey. I thought you might be heading straight home, but that's even better," Kate said. "I made a few calls during lunch break. Would you be free to visit a few apartments with me tomorrow?"

"Yeah, sure." Ellie cast a quick look at Henderson. He was obviously aware of Kate's plans, and from what she could tell, he didn't mind. Of course, it was early on in their relationship—and complicated. Something she could definitely relate to. She remembered that Jordan's parents had invited them to dinner on the same day. "Actually, when are we going to see those apartments? I have plans for dinner."

"Me too. I hope, right?"

"Yep." Derek gave her an affirmative nod.

"All right then. It won't be too late. I made the latest appointment for 4:00 p.m.

"The latest? How many were you planning to look at?"

Jordan who had returned, laid an arm around her shoulders. "Hi."

Ellie had escaped from a dangerous situation, not once but twice. Her friends were there for her, and she actually had a future with Jordan, something that hadn't been so certain in the beginning. She didn't know if she could blame Bethany for stirring up these emotions, but there was still this dark cloud, like a shadow swirling in her mind. The man in the police sweatshirt. Texting her, lying in wait.

What was he waiting for now?

She couldn't even begin to think about scrawny guy and the C4. That case was in the hands of the FBI for the most parts, but all of them would have to work at least a part of the holiday weekend.

"...a few options depending on what we can afford." It didn't register with her until then that Kate was talking to her.

"Wow. Sorry. Say that again."

She caught Jordan's concerned look and shook her head. There was no need to worry about anything. She just needed a moment.

"Anyway, those are good places, close to work and with space for guests."

"I hope not all your guests will have to sleep in the guest room," Jordan said only for her to hear, making Ellie blush.

"Um, okay, that's great to hear," she said. "Thank you, Kate, I really look forward to seeing them. I think I want another drink. Jordan?"

"Yes, sure."

They made their way to the bar, where Ellie ordered another Cosmopolitan, and a beer for Jordan.

"I wanted to say...I'm sorry for snapping at you earlier."

"I understand. It's a lot to take in..." Jordan didn't continue her sentence, just wrapped her arms around Ellie as she leaned into her. "It's okay."

Ellie would chalk it up to sheer exhaustion, but all of a sudden, she had to giggle.

"Okay, help me out here," Jordan said, amused.

"PDAs in front of our colleagues? We've come a long way since that night we had to hide in the bathroom."

"Yeah, and I'm not at all sure you should have another drink, but here it comes."

"You're really okay with me moving in with Kate?"

"I told you, it's a good idea."

There was a different tone to Jordan's voice as she no doubt remembered those moments in the bathroom stall, and funny was not the first thought that came to mind.

"It is, but I'm glad you're taking me home tonight."

Whatever she'd make of this, Ellie was fine with every possible interpretation.

It turned out that none of those possible interpretations was put to action—Ellie fell asleep during the time Jordan spent in the bathroom and didn't wake up until the alarm she had set to meet with Kate on time.

"I'm so sorry." She sighed. "I imagined something different for last night. I think you were right about the second drink. Maybe it was the third."

"That's okay. I need to go in, to see where we are with Wes. We've got five minutes."

"Five minutes are not—" Enough, Ellie meant to say, though she realized soon that a close embrace was all Jordan had on her mind, and she appreciated it. In the beginning of their relationship, there'd been so much pressure, every shared moment borrowed time. They didn't have to continue that way.

"I'd like to buy a new bed, too. Not today, I mean, but once Kate and I found the apartment. You can maybe help me with that."

"I'd love to," Jordan said. "After all, it's for the both of us, right?"

That dark shadow of half-clear memories would disappear eventually, Ellie reflected. They'd been extremely lucky, both of them, and they were building a life together on those second chances.

"Definitely. Do you have time to have breakfast with me?"

Jordan brushed a strand of hair away from her face, kissing her softly. "That depends entirely on how long you want those five minutes to be..."

"Too early?" Kate asked, amused, when Ellie got into the car with her.

"Not what you think," Ellie mumbled, pretty sure she was right. She couldn't help smiling, which Kate would probably interpret as evidence for her theory, but in truth, she and Jordan had saved the best for last. They'd spent more than five minutes in bed though. Right now, between them everything was good and clear. She hoped she wasn't making a mistake.

The first apartment they saw had rather spacious bedrooms for both of them, one of them with a small balcony, and a shared living/kitchen area. A ten-minute drive to work.

"I don't know," Kate said. "The balcony is nice, but it's tiny. I was hoping for something a little bigger, a deck or a patio. We'll have friends over sometimes."

Ellie realized that in all the time in that big apartment, first with Rhonda and then by herself, she hadn't been that much into hosting anyone, kept to herself when she wasn't hanging out with her friends at the *Code 7*. "I like that little balcony."

"Yeah, we'll have to talk about that. If we take this one, we need to toss a coin or something."

The saw three more apartments, and while she was aware the decision would not be an easy one, Ellie felt more confident than she had earlier. This was a step both she and Kate needed to take in order to move forward, a new untainted space that wasn't haunted by previous traumas or sins.

"The one with the balcony, do you think I could fit a King bed in one of those rooms?"

"You have a one-track-mind, Ellie, but yes, you totally could. But, with ten minutes more commute, we could get a big back-yard."

"Do you really want to take care of that? I used to walk home from work, so maybe ten minutes is the limit."

"If I get the balcony, we're all set," Kate promised.

So far, all they could prove was that Officer Wes Martin had delivered some rather sloppy reports, and that he had preferred working one particular neighborhood. All in all, those facts raised some questions, but they hadn't found any connection to Ward or the mysterious man in the PD's sweatshirt...or the one who had possibly used the *Code 7* to stalk his victims. Martin seemed to have come to that conclusion himself, because he had changed his mind on answering questions.

"Hey, I'm sorry, okay? You caught me off guard. My reports might not have been so great, but I've been working lots of overtime. My sister and I are both working hard to keep her in college."

Jordan remembered Ellie mentioning his sister.

"Anyway, I realized how this had to look to you. I can't let her down."

"Okay, Wes," she said. "We've learned a few things in the meantime. Did you ever see a man with a dice tattoo, watching the women there?"

Martin shook his head. "No, not that I can remember. Besides, you guys hang out there, you don't think anyone would have noticed? Who told you that, Danny? He might have made up that guy, to divert attention from him. Some of the girls said he was creeping them out."

"You're talking about Daniel Roth?" Derek asked, frowning. "The owner's son?"

"Well, yes, just because his father used to be a cop, doesn't mean he's cut from the same cloth, right? Ask Miranda and Kelly from the ninth. I mean, it's not enough to arrest him or anything, but he's kinda...strange. They both had the same feeling."

Derek gave her a thoughtful look as if asking for confirmation. Jordan hadn't had enough of an exchange with Daniel to judge him on being strange or creepy, but Roth had mentioned that there had been some interaction with Ward. Had they kept in touch without Roth senior's knowledge? Maybe Daniel had decided one day that watching the female officers wasn't enough. After Ellie was attacked the first time, all employees of the bar had been questioned in case anyone had witnessed anything, but he hadn't been a suspect.

This was the first time Daniel had brought up the mysterious tall blond man with the dice tattoo, and no one had ever mentioned him before. The more they talked to Wes, the more she thought he had some issues which were probably unrelated to the case. His work performance was for Sergeant Bristol to judge. Everything else...

"We'll follow up on this. Can you give us the last names of the officers?"

"Sure. Miranda Clayton and Kelly Hamel. They'll be on the nightshift this weekend, you can ask them when they come in."

"We will. Thank you for your cooperation, Officer Martin."

Back at her desk, Jordan went over the reports Casey and Ellie had filed, the most promising information from a Jay Easton about someone hiring Ward for a job. Scapegoat was probably the best description. They were all connected somehow...and one of them was the yet unidentified buyer of the C4, as well as the man who had taken Ellie from her apartment.

She wanted to talk to Clayton and Hamel herself, and she had to call Ellie too, to tell her she'd be late, and to ask her opinion about Carl Roth's son.

Chapter Sixteen

Her call to Ellie went to voicemail, and Jordan told herself firmly not to go with the knee-jerk reaction. Instead, she texted her and asked to meet at Jack and Pauline's. They'd have to take a few minutes out of family dinner to talk shop.

Speaking of which...she was surprised to realize she hadn't received any texts from Kathryn in a couple of days. Even better. Maybe Kathryn had understood that Jordan was nowhere near ready to let her birthmother be a part of her life. Probably, she had given up—like the last time. There was no point in being disappointed either because that's what she wanted, right?

Officers Clayton and Hamel confirmed Martin's statement, and that there was nothing much to follow up with, though Kelly Hamel had a surprising piece of information: She and Roth junior had gone to the academy together, only briefly, because he dropped out after less than two weeks.

"We already knew each other, so I guess that's why I noticed it more," she said with a shrug. "I don't think he was actually interested in dating me, but he tried to make friends, and really hard. It didn't seem genuine. I heard his dad was a cop, maybe that's the whole reason. He's still trying to make friends."

From the 9th division, Jordan drove home as quickly as speed limits allowed, to change and get to Jack and Pauline's house.

She arrived on time to witness a rather heart-warming scene, Ellie in conversation with Jack and Pauline, sharing a glass of wine. It was a stark contrast to the few awkward moments that had occurred every time she brought Bethany. It was nobody's fault. They didn't click, and maybe that should have told her something years ago. It didn't matter now.

"I see you got started on the weekend," she said, unable to suppress the smile.

"Hey. You made it." Ellie got up to greet her with a kiss. She was wearing a knee-length red dress, the sight warming more than Jordan's heart. Maybe tonight, she wouldn't fall asleep right away...

"Yes—and I'm afraid I need to borrow you for a moment, about work."

Ellie nodded. "I saw your message, but I was already at the door. You didn't see the text I sent back."

"No. Sorry, Jack, Pauline, this won't take long."

"It's okay, Jordan," Pauline said. "Just get a glass for yourself, okay? The bottle is in the kitchen."

"I will, thanks."

In the kitchen, she took a glass out of the cabinet and poured herself some wine. Ellie had brought her glass with her, waiting.

"First of all...you look amazing. It will be really hard to keep my hands off you all evening."

Ellie laughed. "Not that I don't love to hear that, but...You just lied?"

"No." Jordan sighed. "There's something I wanted to ask you, about Daniel Roth."

"Who's that?"

"Carl's son, from *Code 7*," Jordan explained. "I talked to two female officers from the 9th. They said he's been acting creepy around them, keeping a little too close. Did you ever notice anything like that? Did he do the same with you or any female officer you know?"

"To be frank, the guy barely registered with me. He isn't there often, but when he is, he always seems in a bad mood."

"Yeah, I noticed that too. He told us he saw someone else watching the women in the room, a tall blond guy with a dice tattoo on his forearm. Did you ever see anyone like that?"

"No, but..." Ellie looked thoughtful. "I don't know, I think someone once mentioned that dice tattoo, I don't remember where. Wow. That was a while ago."

"Oh no, don't say that. I was kind of hoping he had made him up."

"You think Roth has anything to do with...well, any of this? He knows the guy in the sweatshirt?"

"For all we know, he could be the guy in the sweatshirt. I don't know yet. There is something strange about him, and I take seriously what Clayton and Hamel said."

"Of course."

"Did you know that he attended the academy, quit after a couple of weeks? Hamel was in his class."

"I didn't know," Ellie said. "He seems...I don't know, quiet, when he's there, almost annoyed when someone bothers him by buying a drink. I bet working there wasn't his first choice."

"Yeah, well, all of this isn't a crime, obviously. Martin messed up some reports, but other than that, we couldn't tie him to anything related to your abduction or the C4 deal." Jordan regretted saying this out loud when she saw Ellie shiver and put an arm on her shoulder. "Sorry. I should call Bethany about this and see if there's anything about the Roth family we should know."

"They came to Jensen's funeral."

"Yes, I know, and I don't want to make accusations as long as..."

"I'm really sorry," Jack said, walking into the kitchen. "I didn't mean to interrupt, but if I don't, dinner's going to burn."

"That's okay. I need to make a quick phone call, and I'll be good."

"Did you schedule your vacation yet?" he asked.

"Not yet. We will do that soon. Excuse me for a moment?"

She went no farther than the other corner of the room. Working this closely with Bethany, she needed Ellie to trust her. It took five rings before Bethany picked up.

"Hey. I need a favor. Could you see what you can find on Daniel Roth? And maybe show it to Haynes. If Ward made his deals around the time he was hanging with Ellie's kidnapper, he might remember him. Maybe a name was mentioned."

"Jordan," Bethany said, mildly amused. "Sure I can do that, but not before tomorrow."

"That's fine. We'll check with other sources in the meantime. You let me know the moment you find..."

"Is that all?"

"This is important. Please get to it as soon as you can."

"Okay, this is a bit awkward, but I'm actually on a date. I'll make sure you get what you need. If you excuse me now?"

The next moment, Jordan stood, holding her phone, somewhat speechless in light of the news. She shouldn't be surprised. Bethany deserved to be happy too, and it seemed like they were doing a much better job apart than they had trying for nine years. Bethany had probably tried harder, she had to give her that.

"Is everything okay?" Ellie asked.

"Yes. Perfect. She's going to follow up on this."

"Great timing. Dinner's ready," Jack announced. "Would you like more wine, Ellie?"

"Yes, thank you."

However, when they left for the dining room, she whispered to Jordan, "Don't worry, I'll observe my limits tonight. Because...you know."

Jordan didn't need to hear the words for her body to react. She didn't want to break the spell by asking how the apartment hunt had gone. Come to think of it, she didn't want to talk about it at all in front of Jack and Pauline, and why would they? Everything was fine.

❦

"Did you hear from the young woman who's having the baby?" Pauline asked over coffee and dessert.

"Oh yes. She'll be okay."

On a relaxed evening like this, Jordan didn't think it was necessary to elaborate, how she'd overreacted and felt like crap about it. Pauline could probably read between the lines that Darla had accepted her apology.

"That's good to hear. So...please forgive me, but I need to ask. Have you thought about parenthood some more?"

Jordan almost choked on her wine, while Ellie was quicker to see the humor in that question, even though she had to be blindsided by it. She cast a quick questioning look at Jordan.

"I will chalk this up to the amount of wine you all had before I even arrived. No, we have not talked about this yet."

"It's okay," Ellie said. "I don't mind the subject. The truth is, I haven't really made up my mind yet. I could very well imagine, with the right person...and I believe I found her, but..." She blushed. "Okay, I wasn't exactly prepared. Maybe ask me next time, and I can give you a better answer."

How can you even think about this when you decided not to live with me? The words were on the tip of Jordan's tongue, but she held them back, knowing they would only sound bitter and petty. Ellie had made that decision because Jordan had conveyed to her time and again that she needed space, and how little she'd felt she had with Bethany. However, Bethany was moving on.

"Yeah, I agree," she said, "we'll get back to this another time. We don't exactly have the job schedule to raise children."

"We know that," Jack assured. "And Pauline is only kidding...well, mostly. The subject of grandchildren has come up lately."

"Of course, you decide what's right for you, but...if your decision goes that way, you know that we would babysit anytime."

"Oh boy," Jack said.

"That's right," Ellie agreed. "I think I'll have one more glass—and I promise we'll give this some thought, right, Jordan?"

"We sure will."

She was trying, hard, to be in the moment and not worry about worst possible outcomes, fight the unsettling feeling that the right time was slipping away.

Maybe she should ask Ellie to stay.

***

"I signed a lease," Ellie said, her voice sounding breathless when Jordan could finally let her hands wander underneath the red dress. She hardly missed a beat in her explorations, pushed aside the pang of disappointment. They had decided this together, said it would be good for their relationship. She didn't want to talk about it, just be close to Ellie.

"All right. You're going to show me soon, I guess?"

She pushed the fabric further up and pressing her lips against the warm skin, tracing kisses down Ellie's stomach, finally settling on her knees as she pulled down her panties. Ellie's gasp was somewhere in between surprised and blissful.

"Yes, whenever you want. Kate scored the balcony, but I got the bigger...oh. Room."

"That's good," Jordan mumbled, running her hands up and down Ellie's trembling thighs. "You'll have room for that new bed."

"Definitely."

They suspended their conversation in favor of a more intimate communication, and for all the talk about beds, she took Ellie over the brink before they ever made it to hers.

"Wow, you were in a hurry," Ellie said as Jordan finally opened the zipper in the back so she could undress properly. "Avoiding any awkward subjects?"

"Like the fact that my parents are conspiring about grandchildren, or that I caught my ex on a date when I really had something work-related to say? No. I just wanted you so much."

Ellie looked pleased with her answer. "Well, you have me, and I think all those subjects can wait a while longer...You still have too many clothes on." She didn't wait for an answer, and so Jordan let herself be undressed by warm tender hands. It felt good to be with someone she trusted, with her body, with her fears, and maybe this was an indication of what Ellie had mentioned before—the right person to start a family with. All those thoughts were fleeing rapidly in a wave of pleasure, heated kisses, a deep connection she hadn't felt before Ellie, ever.

It had to mean something. "Please, don't go," she whispered.

⁂

For a moment, Ellie was confused, and then the urgency of how they'd ended this evening made a lot of sense. She held on tighter to Jordan, not wanting to destroy a perfect moment. She felt the need to ease Jordan's mind, though, as much as her own.

"This will be good," she said. "I promise. It doesn't mean that I'm giving up on us, no way. It will give us the time and space to figure everything out, even the baby question. Whatever you're comfortable with. You know, we're doing damn good considering all the shit that happened lately."

"I almost lost you."

Ellie understood what Jordan was going through at this moment, every single detail of it, because she'd felt the same. She had experienced that bottomless fear, even though everyone thought she'd push forward no matter what. She tried hard.

"But you didn't. We're both still here, and we're free to do whatever we want. We'll go on that vacation. We both keep our own space as long as it's necessary, and if you want to sell the house at some point and we look for a new place, you don't have anything to prove to anybody. We'll take the time we need, and you can too, because I'll be here."

After a long pause, Jordan confessed, "I'm a little embarrassed right now."

"Don't be. I understand."

"Yeah, I know you do. Okay. We stick to the plan, go buy a new bed...Would you be okay if we postponed the baby talk for a bit longer?"

"Of course. I want both of the baby's moms to be detectives."

They both laughed. Ellie was filled with a warm, hopeful feeling, though it didn't follow her into her dreams later that night. They were laden with a disturbing mix of vague images, of a man in a sweatshirt stained with eggs, Josh Ward's bloody face and a moody Daniel Roth behind the counter of the *Code 7* watching a blond man with a dice tattoo...watching her.

Ellie woke abruptly, but silently. Beside her, Jordan slept on, and she snuggled into the warmth of her body. Adult decisions weren't always the easiest ones, but sometimes they made a person appreciate what they had even more. She didn't want them to fall victim to a lesbian U-Haul cliché. Keeping her house was something Jordan had done for herself, as a way to slay her own demons, and Ellie would respect that. At some point, maybe after she had passed her exam and they had a clearer idea of the future, they would be able to move beyond. First, they needed to find scrawny guy before he wreaked havoc on the city...and find out what Danny Roth's deal was.

Chapter
Seventeen

J ordan had started the coffee when the doorbell rang, and one
look outside told her without a doubt that she was in for a
conversation she didn't care to have, much less so on a Sunday
morning. If she'd been alone, she might have ignored Jim Larson
until he left, but she didn't want to wake Ellie or explain what
would be rather silly behavior, so she went to open the door.

"Hey, Jordan."

All this cozying up to her, text messages from Kathryn who
hadn't given a damn in decades, now a visit from the man who
wasn't even her father...Not that it made a difference, because
he had never much behaved like one. Whatever these two were
up to, there had to be something in it for them. Jordan couldn't
imagine anything else.

"What do you want?"

"Can I come in?"

"It's early. It's Sunday."

"Jordan, please."

With a sigh, she stepped aside to let him in. "Go ahead. You
want coffee? I think it's ready."

"That would be great," he said, ignoring the sarcasm. "I won't bother you for long."

"Yeah, sure. I appreciate that."

Jordan showed him to the kitchen, where she took a couple of mugs out of the cabinet and filled them with coffee.

"You have a nice place," Jim said. This might have been the longest conversation they'd ever had. Even her relationship with her real father seemed more meaningful, if volatile, in comparison. He, of course, was a criminal, a situation more than awkward for someone whose job was to put those behind bars.

"Thanks. So, what brings you here?"

"It's about Kathryn."

"You're going to what, stay with her, or leave her? I imagine you weren't too thrilled with the revelations." If they could mess with her business, there was no reason why she shouldn't return the favor.

"We've been married a long time. You don't walk away from something like that. We both made mistakes, but...don't you think she has suffered enough? Can't you at least talk to her?"

Jordan shook her head, wondering how they were managing to turn around simple facts so that somehow, she was the one to blame—and it was sneaking into her mind. It struck her as curious that she had refused Kathryn's suggestions while she was sitting in her kitchen drinking coffee with Jim, but it wasn't hard to see the difference. With him, there was little emotional attachment, even less so after she found out they weren't related at all. Kathryn was a whole different story.

"Did she put you up to this?"

"No. I just hate to see her feeling bad all the time. Why don't you give her a chance? She's your mother!"

Jordan took a sip of her coffee, stalling, to make sure she'd choose the words with the most impact.

"Look, giving birth isn't enough to make her a mother, just like being there isn't enough to make you a father. The first years with Jack and Pauline I didn't know whether I should feel grateful, or smothered, because I had no idea what normal parents were supposed to be like."

"It's been a long time. Kathryn hoped that when she helped bring Phil in...and when you came to visit her at the hospital, with your girlfriend, that it might change something."

Jordan cringed at the casual mention of another convicted criminal—obviously, Phil Hobbs had been on a first name basis with Jim and Kathryn. She didn't want to hear any of this.

"What do you think it changes? I understand, it's been a long time, you two might have lain off the drugs for a while and come to some conclusions. Good for you. That doesn't mean I need you in my life all of a sudden."

"What if Kathryn needs you now?"

Enough with the emotional manipulation. "Your time is up, Jim. Nice talking to you. You can tell Kathryn that bombarding me with texts is not helping her case. If I want to meet her, I'll tell her."

He got to his feet, hesitated, and then awkwardly shook her hand.

"Thank you for this. I hope you can change your mind at some point."

I hope I won't.

After she'd seen him out, Jordan returned to the kitchen to find Ellie standing in the doorway.

"That was an early visit," she remarked. "Are you okay?"

"Yes, sure. Kathryn realizes that the text messages don't work, she sends him...It won't make a difference. I have enough on my mind right now."

"I'm sorry."

"Don't be. They'll lose interest soon enough. Are you hungry?"

"I so am. I saw eggs and bacon in the fridge. I could cook that, but I think I'll go for the waffles first."

Jordan had to smile though the conversation with Jim Larson hadn't left her with much of an appetite. "Okay then."

"One time I threw eggs and coffee at the guy," Ellie said out of the blue. "He hardly flinched. I don't know what I was doing provoking him. It took him a long time to bring me food after that."

Jordan was well aware of her dilemma, the push and pull between them, wanting to be there for Ellie when her own story was still too close, struggling to build a relationship on something that had started out as a rash decision. But she believed that at the core, they had something good, something that would enable them to overcome those hurdles.

"I'll never let you go hungry. I promise."

And maybe they weren't even talking about food altogether, but there was one thing Jordan knew for sure—she had to start keeping promises if she wanted to be all that different from Kathryn and Jim.

"I know," Ellie said. "I won't let go either—and I really want those waffles now."

❦

Jordan's complicated parental situation was making Ellie aware of several things—she missed her own parents, and she had pushed down those feelings of grief and loneliness for a long time. She had dealt, had to, because there were no other family members to help her, and she had found solace in the friendship and camaraderie on the job. The recent events had made her vulnerable, and maybe it was also love doing that. Ultimately, it would help her find a way to move forward.

There was no news from Bethany during the quiet Sunday she spent with Jordan. Maybe they had both sensed that this was only the quiet before the storm.

Monday morning, Ellie and Casey had barely pulled out of the parking lot when dispatch called all available units to a familiar address: Shots fired outside of Jay Easton's apartment.

⁂

"I can't be here!" Marla Easton, Jay's wife, cried. "I need to go to the hospital with him!"

"I'll have an officer drive you there," Ellie assured her. "Is there anywhere you could bring the kids for the moment?"

"My mom takes care of them sometimes, but she's at work right now. I already told you, it was Daryl. He came by late last night and yelled at Jay, tried to push him around, but I never thought...You need to find him!"

"What was the fight about?" Daryl, as they'd found out was one of the next-door neighbors, Daryl Fray. He had taken off but couldn't have made it far. Officers were going from door to door at this moment.

"I don't know, I was busy trying to calm down the kids!"

"Okay, Mrs. Easton, this is what we're going to do. Officer Marshall will go with you, and you can tell her everything you remember." Libby nodded. "We'll find Daryl. He'll be held responsible."

"It's about time. He's been terrorizing the neighborhood ever since he got out of prison."

Fray's time as a free man was definitely coming to an end, but was this incident related to the questions they'd asked the previous week? After Mrs. Easton was taken care of, Ellie and

Casey joined their co-workers on the search, until Kate's voice crackled over the radio, "...suspect has barricaded himself in a one-family unit, possibly two hostages inside..."

"Is it Monday or what?" Casey muttered when they hurried to join the unit two blocks away.

Kate informed them that Daryl's ex and her mother were inside the house, all of them in the bedroom in the back of the one-story house.

"No movement so far," she said. "He knows he can't go anywhere from here."

"Yeah," Ellie agreed. "That's the scary part."

⌇

Jordan had just heard of the shooting and subsequent hostage situation when the lieutenant called her into his office.

"Carpenter, I need you to head over to the *Code 7* and assist Dr. Roberts and her colleagues. There's a new development. Troy Haynes made a positive ID on the man who bought the C4, but I imagine that's not a big surprise for you.

Jordan ignored the slight jibe. "Wait, what are you saying? I asked her to look into..."

"Daniel Roth, that's right."

"Ellie's kidnapper and scrawny guy are the same person? What the hell does he want with explosives?"

"Haynes ID'd Roth as the man who came to pick up the C4 in Ward's name. He's missing," the lieutenant said grimly. "Carl let them into the apartment behind the bar. There's nothing new so far."

Almost all of the frequent guests of the *Code 7* were on a first name basis with Roth senior, some had worked with him before he retired to take over the bar. It was probably a dark day for many, but at least it was a big step forward in the case. Sure,

Daniel had plenty of opportunity to observe Ellie, but if he was the kidnapper, why had he chosen her specifically—and what was his plan trying to obtain explosives after she had gotten away from him?

Clayton and Hamel had rejected his attempt at friendship, not that it justified the measures he had taken...Ellie, like most of them, hadn't exchanged more than a few words with him.

"I'll get over there right now."

Meanwhile, the standoff with the hostage taker, Daryl Fray, went on. Jordan wished Ellie wasn't at the scene, but there wasn't much she could do about it now. Contrary to her impulsive outlook on life, Ellie was cautious on the job, not taking any foolish risks. She had to rely on that.

At the *Code 7*, she ID'd herself to the agent in charge and made her way through the empty bar to the small apartment at the back of the bar where Daniel Roth lived. She could tell from Bethany's frustrated expression that the results weren't as hoped so far.

"Nothing to let us know where we could possibly find him," Bethany said. "Despite his many attempts to make friends, Ward seemed to be the only one he actually socialized with. Mr. Roth has no idea where he might have gone."

"He'll emerge eventually. He's not done."

"Oh, so you're the profiler now?"

Jordan held up her hands in mock defense. "Sorry, just a theory. What's his motive? He had to quit the academy, now he hates cops, wants to get back at them?"

"Yes and no," Bethany said, as she leafed through titles on the small shelf next to the bed. "He doesn't like them very much because they do what he couldn't, but he also wants to be close. You know he came to Officer Baker's funeral. He wants a part of this any way he can."

"Then what did he want from Ellie?"

"I don't have all the answers right now, Jordan." Bethany still sounded stressed, though a little less so. "At this point, all we know is that he's the guy we're looking for. He definitely got some of the C4, and as for the abduction, it fits. He was the stalker in plain sight."

"The hostage situation! That's where he's going to go! He wants to be close to cops, Ellie in particular. He likely has access to a police scanner, so he knows she's there right now."

"Jordan, let's not jump to conclusions..."

Ignoring Bethany, Jordan turned around and called Ellie. After three rings, she picked up, barely audible over the background noise.

"Hey. Fray gave himself up, sometime after the ex took a few shots at a garbage can. No one got hurt. How's your day going?"

"Ellie, this is important. Roth could be there. Haynes identified him as the buyer. He's up to something."

"Roth is the buyer? Scrawny guy? And you think that whatever he's up to includes me?" Ellie sounded weary at the thought. Jordan couldn't blame her.

"We don't know yet."

"I think now we do," Bethany said behind her, and Jordan spun around to see her holding up a sweatshirt.

"I don't know what that's going to prove. He borrowed it from me," Carl Roth said, a desperate edge to his voice. "I want to assist any way I can. Danny's a good man. He was so disappointed after he left the academy—which was his own choice, but we all agreed it was better for him. I thought having him work with me here at the bar was the closest he could get..."

"Be careful," Jordan said to Ellie. "Is Doss there? Tell her what I just told you. See if Daniel is anywhere close, better, after you spoke to her, come back to the station."

"Jordan, I can't leave here right now."

"I'll take responsibility."

"I'm sure you would, but I'm sorry, I have a job to do. You're not my supervisor..."

"Then I'll speak to him. This is not the time. Get back and we'll go from here. Don't worry, I'll clear it with Bristol."

Before Ellie could answer, Jordan hung up on her. Bethany's small smile hadn't gone unnoticed with her, but she couldn't bother at the moment.

"Can I see?"

A quick check of the sweatshirt revealed some greasy stains. Eggs.

"Let's get this your lab so your guys can work their magic."

"When time is ticking, we're everyone's friend, aren't we? Mr. Roth, I'm sorry, but we need to go to your office now. Agent Kramer is setting up a trace as we speak. If Daniel calls you, I want us to be able to find him."

"I will work with you, I promise," the disillusioned father said. "God, I don't want Danny to get himself into any more trouble."

Something he had said earlier, registered with Jordan, "the closest he could get," and all of a sudden, the pieces fell into place. Roth thought he was doing his son a favor by giving him a job in the bar. To Daniel, his father had been dangling something in front of him that he wanted badly but couldn't have. She wasn't yet sure about his motive to set up Ward—other than secure an alibi for himself—but there wasn't time to figure this out now.

In fact, she was certain that time was ticking.

"The C4. It must be here somewhere, in the bar. His job is a reminder, every night, that he is not one of us. He hates this place."

This time, Bethany didn't question her instincts. "We'll evacuate the place and get a bomb squad in here. Now!" she addressed Agent Russo who had followed their exchange.

"Where's your furnace?" Jordan asked Roth. He looked horrified.

"What did I do? He had trouble holding a job, and I didn't want him to end up like many of the young men I arrested..."

"I know. Please show me now."

"I'll come with you," Bethany said.

Chapter Eighteen

S taring at her phone, Ellie shook her head. She could read between the lines. Jordan was obviously worried about her. The way she was taking charge—Ellie couldn't deny she found it kind of hot, even when it was uncalled for.

There wasn't much left for her to do anyway, so she was going to head back to the department, risking that Jordan might think she indulged her. Ellie wondered if she'd make good on her promise and involve Sergeant Bristol. She hoped Jordan wouldn't go that far.

"Come on, she cares about you," Casey said.

"I know."

"Don't worry. We'll wrap this up and I'll catch a ride with McCarthy later. You get there ASAP."

"I guess I have no choice." With a sigh, Ellie turned to walk back to where they'd parked the squad car earlier. This was ridiculous. If Daniel Roth knew they were onto him, wouldn't he lay low and try to get out of the city as soon as possible?

She had her answer a moment later when a voice behind her spoke, "Officer Harding."

Ellie recognized the voice, and her hand was on her gun immediately.

"Come on, Ellie, don't do that. I don't want to shoot you."

*I don't want to hurt you...*She was good with voices. She had recognized the nasty threatening tone of Ward's right away. Her only mistake was that she'd never paid attention to Daniel Roth at the bar.

"No, don't shoot. I'm sure we can solve this without any more bloodshed." She turned around slowly to face a man she'd seen many times before he decided to abduct her.

"Daniel. I finally can call you by your name."

"Yeah, whatever, it doesn't matter anymore."

He waved the Glock around, making her flinch. Clearly, he hadn't had much practice, which could mean good or bad for her.

"It does to me. They're on to you now, but I can help you."

"It's too late to help me, or any of you. Now open the door and get in the damn car."

"If I do that, what's the next step? You've been hanging out with cops for most of your life, so you must have an idea of how this works. Right? You paid attention. You know there'll be roadblocks."

"Maybe, but no one's going to suspect you. Now get in there, or I swear I'm going to shoot you!"

"Okay. I get it. I'll drive to where you tell me to, but I think you owe me an explanation, Daniel. Why did you pick me? What did I do to you?"

The door slamming shut sounded like a final sentence. She had to keep him talking, find out what he was up to. There was still the matter of the explosives, after all.

"Now drive."

"Where to?"

"Just drive! It was never meant to be this way. You left me no choice. You shouldn't have run away."

Ellie kept her gaze on the road and her hands on the wheel though she was very much aware of the weapon trained on her.

Roth had an agenda, no doubt about it. So far, he hadn't killed anyone, and that was probably not his intention in the first place. She wanted to keep it that way.

"How did you get involved with someone like Ward? Did he have something over you?"

Roth laughed at her suggestion. "Really, you think he was smart enough to blackmail anyone? I needed him to take care of a few things for me. Obviously, he didn't do a great job, but it's not easy to find a criminal with connections who's willing to do just about anything. I studied up on your cases. A friend of a friend of Tucker Branson's came through, and here we are."

Ellie bit her lip to hold back the angry retort she would have liked to give. He felt so entitled to get his revenge he didn't mind she got hurt in the process, or how badly.

"Take care of what? He nearly killed me."

"That wasn't the plan. I would have stopped him the first time, but Dad made me work. I'm sorry about that. I couldn't be there on time."

"Oh. Wow." What about that other time when she had only a tiny, but fortunately sharp object at her disposal—and for how long could she have fought off Ward, still cuffed to the wall? "I'm sorry, I still don't understand. I mean...It sucks that you couldn't finish at the academy, if that was your dream, but—"

"Shut up!" His shout told Ellie without a doubt that she'd hit a nerve.

"You have no idea. I would be a good cop. You wouldn't have caught Ward if it wasn't for me. But you were all too good to even talk to me. Most of you didn't even bother to ask my name."

"I worked in a bar for one summer. It's not fun, I understand—"

"You don't understand," he protested angrily. "You have everything. You took what you wanted, always, and you had no shame about breaking up another relationship. You don't understand anything."

This was still a sensitive subject. Even as she blushed, Ellie thought she wouldn't sit here and let this self-important guy berate her for having a life. He had screwed up badly because one thing didn't go his way.

"More than you think, but you can still turn this around. I know Ward is the bad guy here. You weren't the one who hurt me. I can testify to that."

"This might be, but it's too late anyway."

"What do you mean?"

"It wasn't supposed to be this way! I was going to rescue you the first time. I would have been the one who stopped Ward and help put him away for good. Now they know it's me, and there's nowhere I can go from here. That stupid bar, always in my way." His voice dropped to a barely intelligible mumble.

"Hold on, what are you talking about?"

To her utter surprise, he laid the gun aside. "I told you, it's too late. Man, I've always hated that place. It will finally be gone."

"What are you saying? That's what you wanted the C4 for? The *Code 7*?"

"It was beneath Dad, and it's beneath me," he said contemptuously.

Ellie's heart was pumping hard. This couldn't be. She needed a way to warn everyone. Jordan was still there, Bethany and her team, many other cops, and civilians starting to arrive for happy hour, or just walking by.

"You know what's beneath you, Danny? Mass murder. You said you didn't want to hurt me. How can I believe you when you tell me you're going to kill all these people?"

She could tell he was troubled. That might be an opening. She had to try.

"What do you mean, these people? There's no one there."

194

"Aren't you listening? The cops are there right now, with your Dad—"

"You're lying! He's not supposed to be there! He's at the doctor's!" he yelled.

"I'm going make a call now. I won't tell them you're here with me, but I'll make sure everyone gets the hell out of there. The bar will still be gone. It's the place you hate, not the people, right?"

No answer. She remembered how his silence had unnerved her in the dark apartment. Ellie wanted to shake him. But first she had to convince him.

"You see this through, no one can help you. We both know you're a better person than that. You stopped Ward. You're a hero, Daniel, and you can still be. Tell me where you put the bomb." It made her sick to say those words, but the means would serve the purpose.

He looked at his watch. "You have ten minutes."

Ellie hit the brakes hard, startling him for a moment long enough to draw her gun.

"Put down your weapon. This ends now."

With Roth disarmed and cuffed, Ellie typed the numbers with shaking hands. Jordan picked up right away.

"You're still at the *Code 7*? It's going to blow in less than ten minutes. Get out of there now!"

The tables had turned quickly. She was breathless with fear for Jordan, and all of their friends and colleagues in harms way.

What if Roth had lied to her and he wanted his fifteen minutes of fame instead of saving anyone? Ellie had a hard time not to cry. She wouldn't, not in front of him. There was somewhere they both needed to be right now.

"How much?" she snapped at him. "Did you plan to destroy just the building, no matter who was inside, or did you want to take out the whole block?"

She would have to bring him to the next precinct, as hers was likely to be in the evacuation radius, but there was somewhere else she needed to go first.

"One bomb. Just the bar. Gone. That's all I ever wanted." There was a blank stare on Daniel Roth's face. He was shutting down.

A moment later, he mumbled something again that Ellie couldn't quite understand. It sounded like "I'm so sorry, Dad."

***

Jordan was at the top of the stairs when Ellie reached her. There was a lot she would have liked to say, but there was no time.

Ten minutes.

Bethany was on the phone, calling in reinforcements.

"Is there anyone in the apartment upstairs?" Jordan asked Roth who seemed in shock. He shook his head. "I use it for storage and some papers—"

"We need everyone out right now."

He blanched even more, but the cop momentarily won over the troubled father. "Backup's on the way?"

"Yes," she said as they were both hurrying towards the front of the building. "Dr. Roberts is taking care of that. We're calling in all units, but for now, we need those people as far away from this place as possible."

On the street, passer-bys were urged to leave the area as uniformed cops taped off a wide perimeter around the *Code 7*. From what Jordan could see, the evacuation of the surrounding buildings was swift, though it had to look like an organized chaos to an observer. The police department was within the determined radius as well.

"Bomb squad's not going to make it in time." Carl Roth wasn't asking. "Damn it, Danny, why?" Jordan had no answer for him as she took him to an area outside the tape where crowds of people were already forming. She wanted to be in several places at once, here, do what she could to help. She wanted to be with Ellie who had apparently managed to arrest Roth. Jordan had been right about him—he had intended to go after Ellie one more time. It didn't turn out the way he'd planned.

Of the ten minutes, there were only two left, but there was no one in the immediate radius. The C4 Roth had gotten away with was likely enough to bring down the building, but everyone, colleagues and civilians, were out of the danger zone.

The wide perimeter of the taped area was hindering commuters, which was a small price to pay, considering. No one would get hurt today.

"Have you seen Dr. Roberts?" she asked a female agent who had come with Bethany earlier. They had gone separate ways after Ellie's call.

"No. I thought she was with you—"

The rest of her sentence was drowned out in the incredibly loud bang that seemed to make the ground vibrate under their feet. They could see the smoke in the distance where the *Code 7* was going up in flames. Roth junior had high hopes, but all he'd managed in the end was to destroy his father's work of over a decade.

Bethany didn't pick up her phone.

They were lucky they'd been able to get everyone out before Roth's self-made bomb blew, but that might not have been his plan. If he didn't intend to murder anyone, he had at the very least casually accepted the potential outcome. Jordan thought with pride that it was Ellie who had convinced him to alert them as to how much time they had left. She couldn't wait to tell her how proud she was of her, but first, she had to find Bethany.

Chapter Nineteen

E llie's first call after the explosion went unanswered. On the next try, the line was busy. On the third, finally, she heard Jordan's voice.

"It's all good," she said, understanding that her being okay was the most important thing for Jordan right now. She felt guilty for being so annoyed with her earlier—for being worried about Ellie.

"Well, considering," Jordan continued. "The building came down, and a few windows were blown out all around. No injuries. Your timing was perfect."

"Thank you," Ellie whispered, breathless with relief.

"Where are you?"

"Not far, I can see the yellow tape from here. I still have Roth with me. Is it safe to bring him in, or should I drive to the 9th?"

"Everyone's going back in. I'll see you there."

Ellie lowered the phone. Everyone had made it out in time. Daniel Roth wasn't going anywhere. The nightmare, the city's and hers, was over.

"The bomb went off," she said to him. "No one was hurt."

"It wasn't supposed to be this way," he repeated. "God, you're all so dense."

"You think so? Well, why don't you enlighten me? You're going to need a damn good story. You drugged and kidnapped a police officer, and blew up your dad's business, because you couldn't do the job you wanted? Talk about dense." She was tired and frustrated, because there might have been a way to stop this sooner, if only she'd remembered she'd heard his voice before. With more time, she might have found a way to convince him to stop the whole idea...If she hadn't managed to escape, he might not have gotten the idea to buy explosives, putting many lives at risk—including Jordan's.

"I was going to rescue you," he said, his features tense with the pain. Ellie only now realized that he had hit his head in her abrupt braking maneuver. She couldn't bring herself to feel sorry for him.

"Yeah, so you told me before. You didn't do such a great job."

"Ward was supposed to scare you, not try to break your skull on that pavement. Later, I told him not to touch you."

A shiver skittered down her spine as she remembered her interactions with Ward, both times. He didn't need a reason, or someone like Roth to pay him.

"Yeah, because it worked so well the first time, right? So that didn't work out, and you went to find yourself some C4 instead. Well played."

"I could be someone," he insisted. "I could be saving lives, if I was a cop."

"But you're not," Ellie said, sick of Roth feeling sorry for himself. "I am."

Jordan found Bethany conferring with the other agent on the other side of the taped area where a multitude of police vehicles were parked.

"Where the hell have you been?" It wasn't until the words were out of her mouth and Bethany gave her a small, amused smile that Jordan realized she'd been out of line. The female agent took her clue from the interaction and ended their conversation.

"I'll call you as soon as I know," she said, and Bethany directed her attention back to Jordan.

"Don't tell me you were worried about me."

"A building we were in earlier blew up, and I hadn't seen you since. Excuse me if I find that a little disconcerting."

"Disconcerting. Okay." Bethany chuckled. "I appreciate your concern. I heard Roth is in custody. I'm curious about what he has to say."

"How about we find out?"

When they sat in the car, she said, "That was quick thinking on Harding's part. I'm not sure I'm happy about it, but I'm starting to like her. She's a good cop. Have you talked to her yet?"

"Not really, I'll be sure to let her know—or you can do it yourself. She's bringing him in as we speak. By the way, thank you for your help on this."

"Not a problem. I'm glad we got him. This is someone I'd like to see go away for a long time. Whiny boy had trouble accepting all the women graduating from the academy when he couldn't. That's pathetic."

Jordan didn't argue.

"For the record, I appreciate it that you care, I really do—so let me return the favor. How are you?"

"You mean because of those ten minutes? I'm not thinking about it right now. We were lucky."

"No, I mean, everything. Dealing with what happened to Ellie...and you, earlier."

Jordan would have preferred if Bethany didn't spell it out in so much detail. When they needed to work together, the results usually spoke for themselves. Private conversations were still tricky.

"Look, I'm not trying to prod or fish for information, okay? So, when I ask how you're doing...that's all I'm asking. I want you to be okay. Even if I'd prefer you could be okay with me, but apparently that's not an option."

"How was your date?" Jordan asked.

Bethany laughed, shaking her head. "None of your business."

"All right then. Here we are."

At the department, Jordan took a quick moment to assure herself Ellie wasn't harmed.

"You got him." That was not the first thing she'd meant to say.

"Yeah. Well, technically, he found me. At least he was almost ready to give himself up." Ellie, already working on her report, rolled back her chair and gave her a tired smile. "I'm glad that it worked out that way."

"Me too. You saved lives today."

At that, Ellie got up from her chair and walked into Jordan's embrace, neither of them caring about who witnessed the scene. Jordan could feel her trembling.

"We're okay," she whispered.

"We are." Ellie leaned into her for a moment. "I have a lot of paperwork to do now. You think you could be back in time to drive me home later?"

"Sure. Otherwise, just wait for me. You'll be okay for a bit?"

"Yeah, Kate is here too." Ellie took a deep breath. "I'll see you later."

They shared a quick kiss before each went back to their own work. Bethany had stayed at a respectful distance. She made no comment, which was fine with Jordan.

Chapter Twenty

"I never meant to harm her," Roth claimed, speaking of Ellie. He had waived his right to an attorney. Carl Roth had hoped to convince him otherwise, but Daniel wanted to tell his story.

"She'd be missing for a few days, I would give you the tip you needed to find her. I had no idea Ward was such a creep."

"Yeah, because what he did to her the first time didn't tip you off in the slightest," Bethany said. It was hard to miss the sarcasm, though it was not enough in Jordan's opinion. She wasn't sure what would reach Roth who had made himself at home in his narcissistic delusion.

"I didn't tell him to do that! It wasn't my fault. I was going to be there, but then I had to work. Scare her a little, rattle her, I said, not put her in the hospital."

"Why go with the same guy then?" she asked.

"Because I managed to find him, and it's not like I know a lot of goons! Branson didn't want to touch anything too hot, but I knew from Easton he was still dealing sometimes, so I tried to make him see reason, and he put me in touch with Josh Ward."

"Tucker Branson, huh?" It was a small comfort for Jordan to see that he might not be all that innocent after all.

"That's the guy. He might have been a better choice, could have got the job done and keep his hands to himself..." Roth sighed dramatically. "I couldn't do all by myself, you know?"

Judging from the flash of anger on Bethany's face, she didn't have any more patience for his antics.

"I still don't get how you went from abducting Officer Harding to pulverizing your father's work. You were angry at him, at the cops who frequented the place, but that's a bit extreme, don't you think?"

He shrugged and winced. "I didn't know what to do! If she hadn't run away, we would have carried on with the plan, and you would finally see what I could do! It was such a disappointment the idiot got himself killed."

"So, you changed your mind after your hostage got away?"

"I had no choice!" Roth insisted. "This was my last chance."

"The bar is gone, and there was some minor damage to surrounding buildings. All in all, not that bad," Bethany said. "What if there had still been people inside?"

"There was a timer. It was supposed to go off with no one inside, I planned..."

"Not to well. And you couldn't have known for sure anyway."

"I'm telling the truth. I didn't think you, or Dad would be there. I was mad at him, yes, because he thought that handing out drinks and adding receipts was all I could do. I needed to put an end to all this, and none of it would have happened if you'd given me a chance!"

"Excuse me? You had your chance. According to Officer Hamel, you didn't make much use of it."

Daniel Roth shook his head with a condescending smile. "You think the people who came to the *Code 7* are the best of the best? Nobody ever sees me, but I hear every single word they say. About your partner's girlfriend. About Harding...well, she had a reputation before I even got in touch with Josh the first time."

Jordan wanted to punch him. The only thing holding her back was knowing that if they kept him talking, he'd continue to dig himself deeper.

"I see. You were listening to some gossip, and that made you decide you'd be so much better on the job."

"They screwed it up with Baker, didn't they? I might have saved him, and then some of your own wouldn't call McCarthy a slut behind her back."

Jordan shared a look with Bethany, shaking her head.

"You still wanted to be a part of it, didn't you? But you couldn't cut it. Instead, you made friends with Ward. We already know your buddy Haynes's side, now tell me how much Branson knew about the job."

This time, they were going to tie up all the loose ends, no matter how long it took.

⁂

"You were pretty amazing today," Kate said as she walked over to Ellie's desk, carrying two paper cups. "This is for my badass soon-to-be roommate."

Ellie gratefully accepted the sweet-smelling caffeinated concoction. She wanted this day to be over, but if she couldn't have that, the specialty coffee would tide her over until the end. She had detailed today's events in her report, and seeing them written in black and white, they reminded her once more what had been at stake.

Jordan had been in that building, some of her colleagues, Bethany. Meanwhile, Roth junior was probably still whining about how his dream didn't come true...Ellie stared at the screen somberly. Maybe he wouldn't have gone to such lengths if she'd handled herself in a different way during her abduction—but they'd never know. It didn't matter. She had done nothing to bring any of it upon herself, Ward's attack, the abduction. Daniel Roth and his late accomplice were the ones to blame.

"Thank you," she finally said. "This is really good."

"I know you have lots of other things on your mind at the moment, but I meant to ask you earlier...Did you talk to your landlord already? I could get a van the coming weekend."

"Oh, they'll be happy to have me out, so that's not going to be a problem." While she was talking, an image of herself, in a nightgown, stealing out of the apartment and then running, flashed in her mind. There hadn't been much of a chance to reason with either of them. If she hadn't taken that chance when it occurred—Ellie didn't want to think of the alternatives. If she hadn't gotten through to Roth when she did...She blinked a couple of times. They were okay. Jordan's words were as much reassurance for the present, as a promise for the future.

"Sorry, yes. Let's do it this weekend."

"After this, you should take your vacation," Kate advised. "It's not like things are going to slow down all by themselves...You still plan on taking the detective's exam, right?"

"Of course. Wow. I can't help thinking...I really wanted this, the job, prove myself. I understand that part. But then he goes all crazy, sending me those messages, breaking into my home so he could come out as the hero, and then what? He wouldn't have made it anyway. Maybe when he realized that he came up with the plan to blow up the bar, everything it stands for."

"I'm going to miss it," Kate said wistfully. "It was almost like a second home."

"I can't help thinking...Did I miss anything, something I could have said to him, how I could have acted differently and make him change his mind?"

"You couldn't have."

She turned around to face Jordan who was carrying a tray with paper cups which almost made her giggle. That would have revealed too much about her current state of mind, so Ellie held back the impulse.

"Why do you say that?" she asked, accepting a cup.

"He always wanted to do something big. He said so in emails and on social media..." Jordan shook her head, sounding weary. "Even though he claims it, in the end we were all means to an end in his delusions of grandeur. The idea that he wanted to be a cop was a story within a story. He wanted everyone to know his name, and it's kind of fucked up that he'll get his wish now. He hated the *Code 7*, everything it represented. You did great. You made him listen, and that gave us enough time."

This arrest meant closure for the both of them in so many ways. It meant Jonathan Darby had never had a hand in the text messages. Ward was who had attacked her on her way home. He was dead. Roth was looking at a long prison sentence.

They could move on. They would.

"Are you ready to go home? I was thinking of packing some boxes tonight, after dinner."

Jordan laughed wryly. "Sure. That sounds like fun."

Doing something as mundane as filling boxes with books, CDs and dishes together went a long way to keep her mind off all the horrible ways today could have ended. They had ordered in and then tackled their task regardless of the time, or the fact that they weren't making too much headway.

Being here with Jordan, watching her work, was all she needed.

Ellie was carefully looking for signs that they were still on the same page, that they still agreed that this was the best solution for them at the moment. Truth be told she was excited to leave the place she'd shared with Rhonda for years, too long after they had both known their relationship wasn't going anywhere. Jordan's house was neat and cozy, but it would always be the house that Darby sold to her while he maintained a torture chamber in his own…Ellie found she had a hard time getting over that fact, even when in the early morning, she drifted off to sleep in said house, wrapped in Jordan's embrace. She wasn't giving anything up, neither of them was. They were navigating the space between them carefully, learning from their mistakes of the past.

All through the week, Ellie kept close, making sure their agreement was still in place. Separate living spaces for now. That was all it meant.

"So, tomorrow is the day," she said when they had turned in for the night on Friday, once again at Jordan's.

"Yeah. That came quickly."

"I've been paying Rhonda's share for too long. And I'm still dying my hair, damn it."

Jordan laughed softly. "You don't have to do it for me, you know. I happen to know your natural hair color."

"You don't say. This is a good change, right? You'll be tempted when you stay over, and we can sleep half an hour longer before getting ready for work."

"I guess you're right. That will be my main reason to stay over."

"Funny," Ellie whispered, pulling her close. "I'll give you another reason."

"I love you," Jordan said, managing to sound breathless in a sexy, sultry way, and very serious at the same time. "We'll take all the time we need, but…I never even thought about having a family, ever. That's because I was never with anyone who wanted to, and for the most part, I thought it was all me. It's all different now."

Ellie listened. Knowing Jordan, she would bring those musings to a halt in a second, starting to feel skittish about going this far...but she could relate, understand how important it was to tread carefully.

"I feel the same," she said. "What I said to Jack and Pauline, I didn't make that up. Not tomorrow or even this year, but if I ever have that, I want it with you. However," she was sure a bit of humor would go a long way to ease Jordan's mind, "First, I want that vacation. No more delay. If anyone deserves it, it's us."

"I was hoping you'd say that," Jordan confessed. "Let's choose another destination though. Better luck this time."

❧

They booked the new trip early in the morning, before their friends arrived to help Ellie move. Jordan hadn't made empty promises—they would be okay. She firmly believed in that, even though she couldn't help feeling wistful as she carried boxes with Ellie's belongings down the stairs to load them into the van Derek had rented. It was the right time for them to be together. In fact, she couldn't imagine anything else, not anymore.

It wasn't the right moment to ask for more, though she had to wonder if there would ever be a right moment, or if what she needed was more courage. She hadn't done so well communicating with Bethany. She wouldn't make the same mistakes, but she needed more time.

Half an hour later, she stood in Ellie's new bedroom after the fifteen-minute drive.

"It's a nice place. Good neighborhood."

She spun around to see Derek standing in the doorway. "Yeah."

They shared a look, and then a wry smile when the realization passed between them that they were likely to see a lot more of each other in their off-time.

She thought of what Roth had said in the interrogation room, and that he got it all wrong. Kate and Derek's situation wasn't easy either, but they had the support of most of their colleagues, like Jordan and Ellie.

In crisis, they did band together.

"I heard you're going on vacation 2.0," he said.

"Oh yeah. Wish us luck."

"I think you've been lucky...and I'm really glad about that."

"Yeah, me too. I could really go for a cold beer now." Jordan's announcement wasn't a complete non-sequitur, as they both didn't want the moment to get too emotional.

"Sounds great. Someone said something about pizza...come on, let's go."

Jordan took a last look at the bedroom, suppressing a sigh. She'd made that bed for herself, and she was going to find out how living apart again would work out for her and Ellie—but first, they'd take walks on the beach in Hawaii, far from all thoughts about past failures—or close calls.

Jordan wasn't a particularly superstitious person—there was no reason to believe that anything would stop them from going on that vacation this time. Still, she couldn't help the feeling—when spending the night at Ellie's new place, or in the morning, when Kate McCarthy drove them to the airport before her shift.

She didn't say it out loud, especially when Ellie seemed to feel the same, her nervous smile telling.

"Come on, guys," Kate scolded good-naturedly as they said goodbye in the drop off zone. "It's going to be all right! Unless you're missing the bad guys already."

"No way," Ellie and Jordan said, almost in unison.

She had to believe that this meant something, that she wasn't pushing away the person that meant most to her just because they weren't living together yet. They had talked about the prospect of having a family. Ellie joined her at dinners with Jack and Pauline. She *was* family. Finally, they were going on this much welcome vacation.

"Who knows? We might even stay there," she joked.

Kate laughed. "I don't think so. You'd get bored, and you know it. I'll be back to pick you up in two weeks. Have fun."

"Thanks." They hugged, and Jordan stepped back to let Ellie embrace her friend as well. "That's the plan, anyway. I guess we better go in now...and you have to go to work. Thanks for the ride."

"You're welcome. See you."

"And here we are," Ellie said when they were getting in line with other travelers. "Can you believe we made it this far?"

"I'm starting to," Jordan said, leaning in to kiss her. "It feels pretty amazing."

About the Author

B arbara Winkes writes sapphic crime drama and Christ-mas romance. She loves writing characters who get the job done, whether it's stopping a predator or saving cherished traditions—while still making time for love. She lives with her wife in Quebec City.

barbarawinkes.com

Also by Barbara Winkes

The Crossing Lines Trilogy
Undercover
Redemption
Vengeance

The Connected Series
Promised to the Queen
Drawn to the Enemy
Tempted by the Protector